FOREVER - PART 1

THE STORY OF LIAM AND ROXIE

LISA PHILLIPS

Copyright © 2024 by Lisa Phillips

All rights reserved.

No part of this book may be reproduced in any form or by any electronic or mechanical means, including information storage and retrieval systems, without written permission from the author, except for the use of brief quotations in a book review.

eBook ISBN: 979-8-88552-179-6

Paperback ISBN: 979-8-88552-180-2

Published by Two Dogs Publishing, LLC. Idaho, USA

Cover Design by Sasha Almazan and Gene Mollica, GS Cover Design Studio, LLC

Edited by Meghan Kleinschmidt of Literary Pearl Editing

ONE

SOMEWHERE OFF THE COAST OF OREGON

Water lapped against the side of the boat. The moon hung like a beacon in the sky, a glimmer of the coming dawn, reflecting what could be. But hope had never done him any favors. If hope had been a worthwhile endeavor, he wouldn't have been left to live out the rest of his days as a dead man.

Angus Dubkowsky scratched at the stubble on his chin, the wind whipping the edges of his collar. That was the name on his driver's license, anyway. Most of the time he went by "Nix," as in a phoenix—the mythical bird that came back from the dead.

He tugged the beanie over his short cut blond hair that also needed a trim, but it wasn't like anyone cared. Those who weren't members of his team that saw him either dismissed him or avoided him, and that was how he liked it.

Made his work easier.

So what if the part of him that wanted to stare at the moon, or the array of stars overhead, never really quieted?

Nix snatched the empty metal cup off the bench beside where he'd been standing. Kai stood at the helm, behind the plexiglass screen, chatting to Dan. The others were down below, standing around the table. They hadn't figured it out yet.

"What do we have?" Nix refilled his cup despite the amount of coffee already sloshing around in his stomach. Above the coffee pot, the guys had taped family photos, old military pictures, newspaper clippings, web pages they'd printed, and even a recipe for brownies no one had ever made. The cupboards were covered so completely that the surface color remained a mystery.

Every family member they wanted to think about, every niece and nephew who won a trophy, social media posts about family reunions they hadn't been part of.

Nix made a fist and knocked his index finger against the one photo that belonged to him, then turned and leaned against the counter while he sipped the tar-like brew.

Ash said, "We have a bunch of nothing."

Ice sat back against the bench seat. "It's going to be impossible to breach. These things are designed to keep people in and they're basically impenetrable."

And yet they'd found the location.

"All this is based on a snatch of intel we haven't even verified." Ash sniffed. "Could be nothing."

"But none of us is going to take that risk," Nix said over his mug. "Because if he gets loose and into the wrong hands, we can all kiss our peaceful lives goodbye."

Two of the guys chuckled quietly, someone else snorted. Sure, their lives were *so* peaceful. But Nix figured they got the idea. Ice had a hole in his shoulder from their last mission two weeks ago, though you'd never know just looking at the guy. He looked ready to move.

The rest of them needed a seminar on healthy sleep habits.

Other than that, they were the top of the food chain and always would be. Thanks to friends, they could move through the world semi-freely. They could be the apex predators they were when life had tried to sideline them into inactivity, which would have killed all of them with a slow, torturous death worse than a blow torch to the sole of your foot. *Ask me how I know*.

Nix glanced around the room. "So how are we going to fix this problem?"

TWO

SEA-TAC AIRPORT, WASHINGTON STATE

Roxie's K-9 could tackle a two-hundred-pound man and subdue him in about three seconds, but it turned out escalators were a big problem. They stepped off the elevator on the ground floor of terminal 2 arrivals into an ocean of people. Roxie gave her a little pat on her head even while the spot between her shoulder blades itched.

She scanned the crowd for one of those "head and shoulders above the rest" guys. Specifically, her husband. Liam O'Connell could power through a crowd like this and send people flying if he wanted to. Thankfully, he opted to use his powers for good. First as a marine, then a police sergeant, and now a cop attached to an inter-agency taskforce.

Pronto, her Malinois, occasionally managed to find her manners, but with her being barely six months old, that was mostly pushing it. People who saw her in a puppy-sized working vest got distracted, like the two kids to Roxie's left.

She held her hand out when they started to rush over and shook her head. "She's working."

Mom got a disgruntled look on her face Roxie decided to attribute to the late hour and a long day of traveling. *Not my job to entertain your kids.*

Roxie had exhaustion of her own after three flights with a dog which had followed sixteen weeks of training to become a US Marshal. Pronto had undertaken a whole lot of basic training of her own with an old colleague of Roxie's from the Marine Corps. Just not intense training, since she was still so little.

Roxie had stayed at the Marshals training center in Georgia long enough to get the star badge in a wallet in her back pocket and then ditched to go pick up her dog. They'd taken two days to reacquaint themselves, and then she'd flown back early to surprise Liam.

Until she reconnected her phone to the internet and realized he was way ahead of her. And here, in the airport.

There.

A couple of groups separated, and she spotted him.

Liam's wide smile flashed. She felt the pull of her own lips, not just about the sheer relief of not having seen him for so many weeks. The one weekend they spent together in the middle had been the only exception. No, that wasn't what had her attention.

His hair. He'd been growing it out when she saw him, and she'd liked the way it fell to his ears. Now it was tied back. She'd hadn't thought she would like that look on a man.

He lifted his chin.

She'd been wrong. She liked his hair *a lot*.

Roxie said, "Pronto, halt."

The dog stopped but remained standing by her side. Roxie reached down and unclipped the leash, but kept a finger curled in the ring. "Ready, girl? Are you ready?"

Pronto strained against the hold.

Liam lifted his fingers and whistled. At that point, she had no choice but to let go as Pronto took off racing down the terminal.

Roxie jogged after her, grinning.

Pronto jumped up and slammed into Liam, who backed up a couple of steps. He held the dog in his arms like a big baby while she licked and chewed on him, looking like she wanted to climb his shoulders. Liam chuckled.

"Pronto, off."

The dog braced off his chest, making Liam grunt, and jumped back to the ground. She circled Roxie's legs and sat on her right side, her body tucked close to Roxie's leg.

"How about you?" Liam patted his chest. "I'm ready."

Roxie laughed, clipping Pronto's leash back on. She gave the dog enough slack so she could lift her arms and wrap them around the back of his neck. Their lips met. She tugged on the ends of his hair. Liam lifted her off the ground because he was a show-off who needed to make a point that he could. Thanks to her training she had at least six pounds more muscle than the last time they saw each other.

He lifted his head, warmth in his eyes. "You're here."

"I missed you, too." She kissed him again, and he set her down. She didn't want to let him go, but taking her attention off a puppy Maligator, even one on a leash with some training, was never a good idea. Least of all in a public—and crowded—place.

Pronto watched the area around them like she was on protection detail. Roxie patted her head and gave her an ear scratch so she'd relax a bit. *Yeah, right.* Worth a try, anyway.

"You look good."

She heard the tone in her husband's voice. "Oh, yeah?" She eyed him, trying to be sultry, but she wasn't a dress and heels girl. She was a cargoes, boots and an assault rifle, sand in her teeth, dirt on her face, mission accomplished kind of girl.

He grinned. "Let's go home."

"Luggage, then coffee, then home."

Liam held her hand, walking with her to the carousel where a few suitcases circled. "Luggage, drive thru coffee you can drink on the way, and then we show Pronto the spot where her crate will live permanently, and you can take your socks off."

She laughed. "Is that a euphemism, Sergeant?"

"What do you think?"

She *thought* they were in public, and out of respect for the people around them, he was going to postpone their reunion until they were home and the dog was asleep. She squeezed his hand.

"Good choice." He chuckled.

Roxie leaned against him and let out a long sigh, releasing all the tension of flights and checked luggage. She was home. Liam had been working on the fixer-upper they'd bought a month after their quick ceremony at the federal courthouse at the end of November. Now that she'd completed US Marshal training, she could work side-by-side with him the way she wanted to rather than get relegated to being in their office at Homeland Security while he traipsed over the northwest tracking dangerous suspects.

"So, I was thinking..."

She lifted her gaze up past his shoulder to get a look at his face.

"I know you haven't spent much time at the house, but there really isn't any furniture to speak of. Just a camping chair and the air mattress I've been sleeping on."

"You didn't buy a bed?" This could get interesting.

He smiled. "I wanted to wait for you and shop together. But what do you say we go somewhere quiet for a week first? Take some time off. Switch off our phones. Reconnect."

"Are you asking me to go on a honeymoon with you?" They'd gone to a hotel on the Oregon coast for a long weekend after the wedding. One of those places with a hot tub on the balcony. Other than that, they'd been working, and then she left for Marshal training.

"Northern California, in the mountains. There's a train tour with a four-course meal, and the place we're staying has great reviews."

He had it all planned and booked.

Warmth swelled in her, even though it would be hard to leave Pronto at home with a sitter. Roxie probably had spent more time with the dog than with Liam since she married him, so there was really no contest.

"I would..." Movement across the terminal caught her attention. "No."

It couldn't have been.

Pronto shifted next to her, on alert.

"No?" Liam's voice faded.

Roxie moved between people, holding the dog leash, following what she'd seen. *Who* she'd seen. "It can't have been him."

"Rox, read me in." Liam strode behind her, and she felt the touch of his hand on the small of her back. "What's going on?"

"I saw..." That was impossible. She couldn't have seen the person she thought she saw. "He's dead. We killed him." She paused long enough to look around.

Liam stepped in front of her, dispassionate workmode on his face. "Who?"

"General... What was his name? We were in Syria." She rattled off a couple of dates, during their second tour on the same squad. "You know, the guy... with the face."

That was probably *super* helpful.

Still, maybe they were on the same wavelength because recognition sparked in his eyes. "Armand Darwish."

"Yes, that guy." She shook her head and glanced around. "I swear I thought I saw him for a second."

"We killed that guy."

"Yes, we did." A dangerous man who had made hundreds suffer because of his actions. It had been one of the times in her life when she'd been proud of her choice to make the world better. That was what she wanted in their new jobs with the Northwest Counter Terrorism Taskforce, but it was still too early to tell if she would get what she wanted.

Sometimes when she thought about all she'd been through, and the journey she'd taken to get here—married to Liam—that in itself had been a mountain to climb. She'd been to hell and back in her life, but things were good. *An embarrassment of riches.* Yet, deep where she'd buried it, she couldn't help the fear that wanted to swallow her.

The terror in her that watched every second of every day with the utmost vigilance for the thing that would snap and make her entire life crumble.

Mostly she tried to ignore it. Then she remembered to pray through it and list things she was thankful for. She would try to distract herself and work it out, pretend it didn't live in her like a bottomless pit of all the things that could go wrong at any moment.

Liam squeezed the spot where her neck met her shoulder. "Let's do a walk-through. Look around."

She nodded, disinclined to compare it to her last relationship. Mark had destroyed her mentally and physically. She'd crawled away from the car wreck that killed him all the way to this life—the one God had planned for her all along.

Liam strode ahead of her, as though determined to be between her and whatever danger came her way. She figured there was a time to be side-by-side and a time for each of them to defend the other. That was what made a relationship balanced, rather than putting one person at a disadvantage.

They completed a circuit of the terminal before she spotted the same jacket.

"Up ahead. In the red ball cap. Green jacket." He could be any other guy, but Roxie had seen that face. She knew that face.

Liam said, "Hang back, I'll circle around."

"Copy that."

He gave her hand a quick squeeze, and Roxie reached under her jacket to unclip the holster that secured her weapon out of sight. She grabbed the wallet in her back pocket and hooked it on her belt. She had planned to get a chain so she could hang the Marshals star around her neck. But if she got in a fight, would it hit her in the face?

Probably.

Maybe that wasn't a good idea. Even if it looked cool, she didn't want some opportunistic fugitive to try and strangle her.

She switched hands with the leash and gave Pronto some praise, and the instruction to stick by her. The dog probably wanted to run after Liam again, and who could blame her after the welcome she received?

Red hat/green jacket shifted. He'd seen Liam to his right, on the other side of the open hallway. He started to turn back toward her, and Roxie saw his face.

It was him.

Disbelief warred with surprise in her, nearly faltering her steps while she dealt with the shock of what her eyes couldn't quite believe. She sucked in a breath, and beside her, Pronto shifted. The dog was reading her.

Darwish spotted her, and a muscle flexed in his jaw. He ducked to the right—her left—and used a keycard to disappear into a side room off the hall.

"Come on." Roxie ran to the door, whispering a prayer in her heart that she would get there before the door clicked shut.

Liam was right behind her.

Pronto ducked through the door. The leash slipped out of Roxie's hand, but she grabbed the door before it closed. Liam caught it above her head. "Go."

She raced into a hall that ran parallel to the terminal hallway after her K-9. "Pronto, heel!"

The dog ran after the man, who slammed into a door at the end. He fumbled with the handle, spotted the animal bearing down on him, and kicked out with a heavy boot.

Pronto yelped and fell to the ground.

"No!" Roxie ran to her.

General Darwish disappeared through the door.

THREE

Roxie reached over and squeezed Liam's knee. "Maybe you should tell me what you did to the house."

He didn't quit bouncing his knee. Maybe he should talk and think about something else.

After Liam carried the dog to his SUV he'd spoken quickly with the airport police department. When he'd explained their pursuit of a dead man, the cops hadn't seemed overly worried that some guy who may or may not be anyone dangerous had been spotted.

It was more because of the fact the guy had gained access to a secure area of the airport—as had Liam and Roxie—that seemed to be the problem. So the airport police were going to follow up with Dakota Pierce, the Homeland Agent who was their boss.

Liam never worried about fighting his own battles, or doing all the work himself, but he also knew it was his supervising agent's job to coordinate. Especially if something came up while Roxie and Liam were on their week off.

Did Roxie still want to go?

He'd been trying to ask her to go away with him for a week, and she'd said no. He'd been taken aback at first, before he realized her attention was on something entirely different. He couldn't believe she'd spotted that man. A guy they'd undertaken an operation to eliminate. As much as people wanted to believe things could be resolved peacefully, sometimes force had to be used.

They'd saved a lot of lives taking out General Darwish and freed a lot of people who got to continue their lives under the authority of his half-brother, who chose not to victimize people he should be protecting. Until it turned out that wasn't true.

She shifted in her seat beside him. "You're supposed to be distracting me."

They had chosen a couple of chairs in the corner of the 24-hour emergency vet since Pronto's doctor was closed at this time of night. Liam bounced his knee.

"Maybe I need to distract you." Roxie touched his cheek and turned his face to her. "She wanted to walk on her own. She walked around in the back of the truck before she got in her crate."

"Doesn't mean she's not hurt."

"That's why we're here." She touched her lips to his.

Liam tugged her over. "Sorry we didn't get to go straight home and relax."

"On your *air mattress*." Her eyes flashed with humor.

"Okay, so I probably could have bought a bed." Truth was, he wanted to do all that stuff with her. "The house looks great." He'd been cleaning every corner and every surface for days, trying to distract himself while he waited for her arrival. Then he'd bribed their old friend who'd been training Pronto to tell him her travel plans and found out she was coming home early to surprise him.

Liam liked surprises. As long as he had full knowledge of the impending event.

"You fixed up the bathrooms and the kitchen and stuff?"

"Replaced the roof. Re-did the floors with tile and underfloor heating in the kitchen, so when you get up during the cold months, you won't have to put socks on. The back of the open plan living and dining area is now a wall of window panels that let the light in. You can unlatch it and slide the whole thing back like a partition door with multiple panels that go together like an accordion. So that the back is just...open to the yard. Pronto can run in and out, and you can sit and watch her play."

He'd also repaired the fence in multiple spots, reinforced everything, and switched out some of the shrubbery for more dog friendly stones and steps that Pronto could run around and jump up and down from. It looked like it could be a garden, but it was basically a dog exercise area.

Liam continued, "I pulled out the old tub/shower thing and put in a tile walk-in shower. Heated towel rails. That one was tricky, but Rory came down from Alaska for a week and helped me do that. Conrad came over from Benson a month later and helped with the floor."

He wasn't sure what it was with his brothers, but they'd opted to come at different times rather than in the same week so they could all hang out together. Whatever went down between them had happened while Liam was deployed with the Marines—hanging out with Roxie. Taking down dangerous terrorists and enemy combatants like General Darwish.

The inner door opened and the vet working tonight strode out.

Liam and Roxie both stood, and he felt her fingers slide between his.

"X-ray is done. I took a look, and she has a cracked rib."

He felt her let out a breath.

The doctor said, "I've wrapped her chest, and I'll get you medication to keep the pain at bay, but she needs to be convinced to get as much rest as possible."

Roxie chuckled, letting out a little sigh. "Right."

The doctor smiled. "She tried to hop off the table. If she's moving too much, cut the meds to half so she can feel it a little, or she'll be in a much longer recovery."

Roxie said, "Got it."

"Crate her for at least two days, except bathroom breaks and eating. Lots of rest after that. And bring her to your vet in four weeks for a follow up to see how she's healing."

"Thanks, Doc." Liam held out his hand, and the doctor shook it before she shook Roxie's.

The doctor went to get Pronto, who meandered into the waiting area with the vet tech holding her leash. Roxie moved slowly. Liam could tell she pulled back her speed so the dog would take the cue from her.

Roxie knelt, and Pronto moved all the way in, touching the top of her head to Roxie's collar bone.

She rubbed the dog's neck and head. "Let's go home, yeah?"

They stepped out together, heading for his SUV. He scanned the parking lot even though they weren't working. He might be able to turn off the threat assessment someday. He might be able to let go of the need for vigilance long enough to not be in protective mode constantly. But then again, the more time he spent with Roxie, he figured that might be unlikely. Especially if they had kids someday, becoming more than working-dog parents.

She got Pronto settled in the crate again. "Home?"

Liam hit the button to close the rear door, and they both stepped out of the way. "Dakota was expecting us, and we could update her on the General." She probably didn't want to leave town now their dog was injured.

Roxie nodded. "You pre-booked everything?"

He didn't care about the money, but he did want to tell their supervising agent about the dangerous man they'd seen. "Josh and Neema are in Southern California on a DEA case, so she's alone for at least another ten days. She jumped at the chance to spend time with Pronto. She even said she might work from home. And that she could send photos every day like those dog watchers on that app."

Roxie gave him a half-hearted smile.

They had no furniture in their house. He didn't want to think of it being a metaphor for where their marriage was at after five months. But it couldn't be denied it was time to color in between some of the lines. Make good memories, honeymoon as she'd said, and just *be* together.

She lifted up on her toes and kissed him. "Dakota will make sure the General is found. We can baby Pronto when we're back."

Liam frowned. "You still want to go?"

"Life doesn't always go how we planned. We, of all people, know that." Roxie shrugged. "Pronto might get more rest if we're gone than if we're at home or working."

He drove them to Dakota's townhouse—the one at the end of the row with the big yard for her husband's DEA K-9. Liam had texted their supervising agent a few times in the waiting room and filled her in. When he pulled up out front, Dakota opened the door.

Older than Liam, though she didn't look it, Dakota Pierce the Homeland Security agent was Dakota Weber at home. Like right now, wearing socks, black skinny pants and an oversized sweater with her jet-black hair down. "How is she?"

Liam called out, "Cracked rib. She just needs rest and meds."

Dakota chuckled. "A maligator resting? That's funny."

Roxie led Pronto over by her leash, smiling. Clutching the white paper medication bag in her other hand. "Hi."

"You're back, Marshal." Dakota smiled. "And you already want to open a case?"

Roxie shot a look at Liam as they stepped inside.

He went back for the dog crate and hauled it inside. Pronto walked over to the dog bed in the corner, wagging her tail. "Looking for Neema?" He set the crate down where Josh kept his when he and the dog were here and left the door open.

Pronto sniffed the bed, then trotted to the crate and laid down inside with a slump, a groan, and a loud sigh.

Roxie returned Liam's smile with a gentle one that was purely her. She looked as exhausted as the dog.

Dakota hit the power button on the laptop she had open on the breakfast bar. "This the guy?" A photo illuminated on the screen, an old military file. The word *TERMINATED* across the man's face.

"Yes, that's him." Liam walked over. "General Armand Darwish."

"You're both listed in the operation personnel report."

"Pretty sure Liam's the one who wrote that report." Roxie scrolled down on the mouse. "So many years ago. Pretty sure we were kids at best, traipsing around the desert strapped with weapons."

Liam squeezed her neck. "Good times."

They'd met in the Marine Corps, and regulation had kept them from doing anything about how they felt for each other. He'd come home to Benson, Washington, after his father passed and became a cop. She'd left the Marines and been sucked into an abusive relationship with a guy they'd served with.

When she showed up in Benson the summer before, he hadn't been able to believe it was her. After her ex's brother came after her for revenge for the accident that nearly killed her too—which had been the plan, for them both to die together—Liam had helped protect her.

Then he married her.

Now they worked together on a federal taskforce,

and she'd opted to become a Deputy US Marshal so they could go out into the field together.

Liam frowned. "I don't understand how he's alive. I mean, it was him, right?" He looked at Roxie even though he'd seen the guy, too. "We killed him. How is he walking around the airport?"

Roxie shook her head. "I couldn't believe it when I saw him."

"So we track him down, then, I guess." Liam paused. "If we can figure out how to find him after he disappeared in the airport."

Roxie said, "Maybe the security office has been able to track him down."

Dakota smiled. "I'm glad the team is back together. But I want the two of you off the next week." She looked at him. "Take your trip. I'll watch Pronto. You two need to rest."

Before either of them could raise an objection, Dakota said, "We don't do burnout on this team. You both need to take some time off."

Liam nodded. "But you're on the Darwish hunt, right?"

"I'll open the case and see what comes up. As soon as you guys get gone, I'll call the airport." She looked at Roxie. "Leave a shirt of yours, preferably dirty. I'll put it in Pronto's crate so she can smell you nearby."

"Thanks." She looked relieved and exhausted as she relayed the information from the vet and then sat with Liam while he got Pronto's duffel with her food, bowl, and toys in it from the back of the SUV.

They were really leaving? Going on vacation when a dangerous man was out there?

"Liam."

He turned back to Dakota.

"The team will work this while you're off, and as soon as you're back, you join. Got it?"

He had a sneaking suspicion that was an order related to his inability to switch off. Roxie went to the crate and laid the shirt inside, petting Pronto before she clicked the door shut. Pronto snored lightly the whole time.

Then she squeezed his arm. "Let's go." Back outside, he held the door for Roxie while she climbed in. "Feels like leaving your kid at grandma's, right?"

Liam shook his head. "If anything happens, we can come home right away. We won't even be a day's drive from here."

"With the search for Darwish or Pronto?"

"Either. Both." He shrugged, not wanting to admit he didn't like leaving a loose thread at work. But when did things settle down enough to take off with nothing pending?

That didn't really happen in their line of work.

Which was why they leaned on each other, and the team pulled together so that they didn't work all day every day of the year. Everyone needed a break, and that was especially true for the two of them right now. When Josh got home, Dakota would spend time with him before they came back to work. The other couples on the team consisted of their NCIS agent, Niall and his wife who was pregnant with their third child. Talia, their NSA tech whiz had married a Secret Service agent who worked across the street at a different federal building. They also had kids.

Everyone knew what it was like to have personal responsibilities and those latent workaholic tendencies. Which was why Liam had figured they came to the right place deciding to take the job offer with the Northwest Counter Terrorism Taskforce.

"Come on, Sarge. Let's go home." She tugged her door shut, and he jogged around the hood.

She was right. Life didn't always go the way anyone planned. What was the verse he'd read just a day or so ago? It had stuck in his mind. Something about man planning his way but God establishing his steps.

Liam restated it in his mind as a prayer while he climbed in. That was another thing he'd worked on while Roxie completed the long training course. He'd started to read his Bible and pray every day. To let God establish his steps by sticking close to Him the way his dad had shown them all how to do.

He turned on the engine, and she leaned over, kissing his cheek. "Love you."

"Enough to leave your injured dog with someone else and go on vacation?"

"We're not abandoning her." She chuckled. "And we can't take her everywhere with us her whole life."

He was glad she was amenable to alone time. Something that would start right now, continue tomorrow on their trip, and hopefully be a regular thing of recharging together from their busy lives.

He really should've bought a bed.

FOUR

Two days later

"How is she?"

Roxie looked up from her phone to see her husband's soft face. The train rumbled out of the station, getting started on their journey through this hilly area of Northern California. "Dakota installed a camera facing the crate and Talia gave me the log in to access it. She's still sleeping."

Her dog had been up at six, taken meds and eaten, and then returned to the crate to sleep for another three hours. Dakota had taken her for a short walk after that and would again a couple more times at least before the end of the day. It was better than Pronto thinking she could run about.

"That's good." He sipped from the bubbly drink in the tall, slender glass in front of him. "Better than this drink."

Roxie chuckled, stowing her phone away where

she would feel the vibration but otherwise not be disturbed. She'd turned off nearly every notification except anything from Dakota.

The server passed by, and Roxie lifted her finger. "Could my husband have a cup of coffee?"

"Absolutely, ma'am. No problem. I'll get that right now." The server swept down the train car to the bar at the end.

She'd wondered if they wouldn't have anything to talk about other than work, but so far, she hadn't had reason to be concerned they didn't know how to relate to each other. All the time they'd spent on the phone while she was in Georgia meant they might lapse into comfortable quiet, but sooner or later one of them would pick up the conversation again.

Enough she could with all good conscience ask, "Can you even believe General Darwish might've survived our attack?"

The server set a cup on a saucer and shot Roxie an odd look. Liam waited until she was gone, then said, "We had proof he was dead. Or as close as we could get since the guy was vaporized."

"What are you thinking?"

"Lookalike. Someone who got plastic surgery to look like him. Or the double was the one we chased, and we had no idea it was someone posing as him."

Roxie didn't like any of those options. "We had no idea. He probably laughed himself sick."

"If he is in Washington, he has to be using a disguise to get around. Especially since he knows now that we recognized him. Whatever he does next won't be good."

"Did Dakota get any leads?"

Liam said, "She's still tracking down the car he drove away in."

The airport security personnel had tracked the Darwish lookalike to the staff parking garage where he'd left in a white compact. They'd only gained a partial license plate, and the most likely match had been stolen from an elderly woman's storage unit the week before.

"You don't get a fake access card to airport employee areas just for fun. He had to have a reason to need access."

Liam nodded. "There's no 'chatter' according to Talia. No indications online or anywhere else that anything is in the works. No whispers about our deceased general."

"So they're the most tight-lipped accomplices *ever*. Great." She sipped her drink. "I'd rather go shoe shopping than work a case with no leads."

"That wouldn't be a good distraction. You take ten minutes to buy shoes."

Roxie shrugged. "I either find what I'm looking for, or I don't."

"Maybe we should find some home goods stores while we're in the area, and we can *browse*."

Roxie mock-shuddered. "Throw pillows and lamps?"

"We can't sit on my one camping chair for the rest of our lives."

She sipped her bubbly drink. "Watch me."

Liam laughed. It was a good look for him, and she loved being the one who put amusement and the light of enjoyment on his face.

"So, your brothers came and helped with the house—which is amazing if I haven't said that yet."

He smiled into his coffee cup. "You might've mentioned it a couple of times."

"The shower tile is *inspired*."

"Okay, okay. Move it along."

Roxie said, "How is your mom doing?"

"Dating Bob Davis of all people." He shook his head. "But they seem happy."

"Well, yeah. Bob is great." He'd been her supervisor in the Cold Case Department at Vanguard, and they still emailed regularly. She had a text thread with the twins Peter and Simon Olson, who also worked for the private security and investigations company.

In fact, she'd passed them the information she'd found out about General Darwish and asked them to put out feelers. See if anyone they were connected to had heard word about a Syrian death dealer back from the grave.

She might be a federal agent, but old habits died hard, and the people at Vanguard had some serious skills.

Liam shifted in his seat. "Actually, Mom didn't take it so well when she found out we got married at the courthouse right before we left and didn't tell anyone." He winced. "She went on a rant about at least having a party and letting everyone give us housewarming presents."

"Huh. Maybe we could do that after we buy furniture. Get everyone to come over for a party." She looked out the window at the rolling hills on their side of the train car as they chugged past at a moderate speed and the seat rumbled under her. "Celebrate a little when things settle down."

"I'm not sure things will ever settle down in our

lives." He smiled. "But I was thinking of something more planned than a backyard party."

Why did she get the feeling this was something important to him? Liam rarely asked her for anything. He'd been this well of calm in her crazy life. It seemed like he weathered whatever came at him like an old oak, putting down deep roots.

He cleared his throat, lacing his fingers on the table between his place setting. His wedding band was dark gray silicone, where hers was blue. His fingers shifted, and she saw a white gold diamond ring in the palm of his hand. "I was thinking..." He almost seemed nervous.

Roxie sat waiting, soaking him in, astounded he might ever be nervous about anything. She already had a ring. Why had he bought her another?

"Maybe in the summer, we could renew our vows. Have a kind of wedding somewhere in Benson with a church service and a reception. Dancing. Cake."

She'd already worn a dress and said, "I do" to him. But as with everything with her husband, there was an intoxicating temptation to say yes to whatever he asked. Mostly she jumped without looking, knowing he would catch her.

Only in becoming a US Marshal had she taken a step of independence and created a lane for herself, so she didn't have to live in his orbit while he saved the world.

"You want to get married again? For real?"

Liam said, "I wouldn't change how we did it. Not for anything."

"And this isn't about your mother?"

Liam shook his head. "What do you say? Will you have a summer wedding with me?"

He'd bought her a ring, and here he was, across the table on this special trip, looking all nervous and bearing his heart to her. It was like catching a snowflake. But those inevitably melted.

Like the dreams she'd always had, where her father walked her down the aisle. Where she didn't have worries and fears.

She'd grown up enough to realize they weren't real.

These days, Roxie lived in a place where reality met hard work and joy was what you carved out for yourself.

"It'll be a lot of money doing all that. For something that's a one-time event, and not even an amazing week-long getaway break." Roxie smiled, but even she didn't believe it.

She didn't know how to say that it wouldn't feel right to her to do it all over again. Even for the sake of family—his. It would never feel like the dream she'd had, the one she gave up when her father died, and then her brother. Because what did she bring to this relationship? Still she wanted to snatch that ring out of his hand and slide it on her left hand to sit with the band, but that would only give him the wrong idea.

Even if she wanted that more than anything.

Enough that she had to pull her hands back and clench them between her knees to keep from jumping him, she wanted that ring so badly. Roxie wanted every part of belonging to Liam O'Connell, the first family she'd had in decades. The first man she'd fallen for, and the last one she would ever love. Life might have tried to get in the way between those two, but they were on the right path now.

"Maybe just think about it this week." The ring went out of sight in his hand. "Can you do that?"

Roxie nodded. A first course of a light eggs benedict breakfast was delivered, along with a refill of the bubbly. But getting happy and tipsy wasn't going to keep everything from still hanging in the air around them. She was too much of a cop to not have her wits about her.

"Also, you should think about letting loose a little." He motioned her toward the window and got up. "Scoot over." Liam slid in beside her, and she leaned against his arm, which he laid across her lap to hold her hand. "You're on vacation. You are allowed to switch off."

She clung to his arm and stared out the window. "It's been a long time since I did that, and it didn't end well."

His lips touched her forehead. "You're safe with me."

She closed her eyes, surrounded by the feel of her husband. "You should've seen me a week ago, kicking in doors and taking down bad guys."

His chest rumbled with amusement under her cheek. "I like both Roxies. The one who needs me and holds on tight, and the one who don't need nobody because she'll kick butt and take names before breakfast."

"Especially if I haven't had coffee." She chuckled with him, but inside, that well of fear seemed to rumble and bubble. Like a volcano getting ready to erupt.

Her heart had skipped a beat when Darwish

kicked Pronto. If anything happened to the dog, it would be just like in high school. Her boyfriend had backed out of the driveway too fast, spun around, and hit her dog on his way out. He hadn't even stopped.

She'd had to bury her best friend. The dog her brother left behind when he deployed—and then never came home.

Her father had drank himself to death.

Her mom... She hadn't seen the woman who birthed her since she started kindergarten, but none of the memories she had were good.

She'd lost her brother...then his dog.

The military had been her family and her home for years. Then she'd traded freedom for a different set of chains that left her bleeding on the roadside. She'd contemplated her faith a lot while she'd been gone. Through lonely nights in a twin bed, far too similar to basic training, wrestling with Jesus being her Savior, and not setting up Liam's role in her life as the same thing. She had to have each separately, devotion to her Savior and love for her husband. Each fulfilled different functions in who she was. The last thing she needed was to get to a place where Liam became everything to her, and she lost sight of the right way things should be.

Liam was a gift of God she didn't plan to squander.

The train started to decelerate. The car jerked in a way that made the server spin around from the liquor shelf with a confused look on her face.

"Huh." Liam shifted.

Roxie sat there, content that her husband would protect her no matter what happened. And when he needed a teammate to kick a door in? She would be there. After their vacation.

Roxie lifted her phone and illuminated the screen. She had no new movement notifications for the camera, which meant Pronto was still asleep—so she didn't need to worry. Her dog was resting.

The train jerked.

A bottle fell from the shelf and shattered on the floor. Someone screamed.

Liam twisted away from her.

Roxie looked over his shoulder down the train car just as an orange ball of flames ripped through the back of the car. The thunder of a detonation cracked through the air, eclipsing everything in an earsplitting eruption of noise that swallowed the train car.

Liam shoved her shoulders down and cried out, covering her with his body. The whole world flipped upside down, flinging them apart.

She grasped for him but felt nothing.

Then her body slammed into something unyielding, and everything went black.

FIVE

Liam's first thought when he regained consciousness was of Roxie in a white dress. Not just any white dress, mind you. The kind she might wear if they'd had a big fancy wedding with all their family and friends standing around. Smiling so much it hurt. Eating and drinking to celebrate. Dancing all evening.

She'd worn a white dress at the courthouse, the kind she could wear in the summer with flip flops and she would look casual. If the woman ever wore dresses. Right now, that dress was at the back of her side of the closet—which he hadn't renovated yet. Though he had poorly sketched ideas for different shelves and rails for clothes. Places she could put shoes—double height because it would mostly be boots.

His second thought was that his body didn't feel right. His shoulders ached, and one leg was contorted oddly in a way that made his hip burn.

He gritted his teeth and tried to focus on the world around him.

Smoke laced the air, and his eyes felt like he'd

been hit with a handful of gravel or sand. He pulled his legs back toward his body and ignored the burn in his hip. *Ouch*. It wasn't worse than wearing SWAT gear on his vest for years and the degenerative issues he'd have to deal with as soon as he quit police work.

He lay on his side, on what looked like the side wall of the train.

Roxie lay a couple of feet away, already stirring.

He pushed out a breath and crawled to her, because standing would take too much energy right now. His chest hurt like he'd been hit by a linebacker. Liam used his elbows, dragging himself across the ceiling of the train.

Someone screamed somewhere behind him, and it quickly dissolved into crying and whimpering.

They needed to help people.

Roxie patted her pockets and around her. "Phone. We need a phone. We need to call for help."

He slammed his mouth on hers. It wasn't gentle, the surge of relief they were both alive and ambulatory rushed through him like an instinctive thing. Roxie clung to him. Which was good, because if she'd shoved him away, he'd have had to force himself to let go of her and back off. Instead, she absorbed all his relief as though it was what she'd been born to do.

Which he figured was true.

When Liam managed to pull his head back, she shoved her face in his neck and held on for a second. He felt the grasp of her hands. Then she let go just as fast and dug in her pocket.

"911." She shoved her phone at him. "Now, Marine."

Liam blinked at the screen. She scrambled up, moving around him as she got to her feet. Liam pretty much fell back, turning to watch her move through the train car.

"My name is Roxie. If you can hear me, call out!"

Someone cried to her. She bent around a seat and spoke with someone, but his ears rang so he couldn't hear what she said.

Liam looked down at the phone. Her phone. He used her code to unlock it, since they'd swapped codes months ago. He had nothing to hide on his phone, and she'd told him she didn't either. It just wasn't that big of a deal for them to have "privacy" on their devices, since hiding things from each other rather than being upfront had never worked for them. Other couples could do whatever they wanted.

"...what is your emergency?"

Liam's ears quit ringing enough he could hear. "The train exploded." He blinked a few times and focused his thoughts, explaining what the train was and how many people had been on it—near as he could figure. Whereabouts they might be.

"Are you a police officer?"

"Sergeant Liam O'Connell, but I work up in Washington State." He had to cough, smoke laced the air. Had that been there before?

He looked around. Was something on fire?

"Rox!" She was currently helping an elderly woman and the woman's husband back toward him. They needed a way out. "We have to get out!"

The last thing he wanted was for them to survive an explosion only to be burned to death in a tragic fire. What a waste.

"Sir?"

Liam said, "The train is on fire. We need FD, PD, and as many medics as you've got. As soon as you can get them here." He hung up the phone and stowed it in his pocket, clambering to his feet. *Ouch.* He ignored that same burn in his hip. As if he had time to be injured. He could worry about that later.

Roxie held the older woman's arm steady. The husband had blood running down his face. She said, "Help me get them out. There are lots more we need to assist."

"We need a door."

The older man muttered, "Or a hole in the train."

"Between the cars we should be able to get outside." Liam held the older man's arm and walked him to the doorway of their car. Between the two, the bridge that normally would've allowed people to move safely between cars had torn away like kitchen foil.

The sun beat down overhead, making him blink against the sudden brightness.

He helped the older man onto the grass. The guy turned and helped Roxie with his wife.

Liam said, "Get clear of the train and find a spot where people can come to you. We need one central area, close but not too close, where emergency services can find you."

"I can do that." The older man nodded, holding his wife's elbow.

Roxie held out her hand to Liam. He clasped her wrist, and she hauled him onto the train, letting go as she turned to the inside. She moved quickly, down to a seat a couple of rows behind where they'd been, where she crouched.

Liam went past her, finding the server crumpled in a heap on the floor in the corner. Her shoulder had to be dislocated to be hanging like that. He checked her pulse. "Good thing you're unconscious, or this would hurt." He gathered her into his arms and carried her out.

The older couple had sat on the grass, and the woman leaned against her husband.

Liam laid the server close, tucking her arm to her side. "Any sirens yet?"

The man shook his head.

"I'm Liam."

"Cecil. This is Maryanne."

Liam touched his shoulder. "Nice to meet you."

When Liam turned to look at the train, he could've been entirely distracted by Roxie hauling out a young woman with blood running down her face. But it was the end of the train car that caught his attention.

Five cars, and the engine first. The open-air car toward the front of the train was on its side with people climbing out, helping one another. The car they'd been in was the fourth.

Car five, which he thought might be the kitchen and staff area, was nothing but debris. The back of their car had been hit, turning them on the side.

Had to be that there was an explosion in the kitchen. Maybe an accident with a gas line.

The woman Roxie was helping yelped.

Liam jogged to them and saw another woman stumble out of the train behind them and fall to the ground. He caught her arm and slung it over his shoulder. They helped both women to the spot beside the older couple.

A uniformed train company employee jogged over, his slick hair mussed and his eyes glassy. "What happened?" His eyes took in the wreck at the back of the train, disbelief that looked a whole lot like shock on his face.

"We need to get everyone out to the grass," Liam said. "In case there are any secondary explosions or fire."

The man blinked.

"What's your name?"

"Carlan." He shook his head, but it dissipated nothing from his expression. "We were dancing, and everything just...flipped."

Liam nodded. "I need a headcount on passengers from you. Who is off the train, who do we still need to find. Can you do that for me?"

Carlan sucked in a breath. "Are you some kind of cop?"

Okay, so even when he wasn't working, it was obvious to people around him, because that was twice now someone had commented on it. "Liam O'Connell. I work with Homeland Security. This is Deputy US Marshal Roxanne Helton. We aren't working here, we're just helping. All right?"

There were people to assist, so they couldn't stand here talking for long. Several people were disembarking the train on their own, but there could be people still trapped.

"Okay." The guy nodded and hurried off, looking unsteady on his feet.

Roxie leaned against him for a second. "Actually, it's Deputy Marshal O'Connell."

Liam turned to her, frowning.

"I got them to draw up name change paperwork, and I signed so it's all official."

She'd taken his name? They'd married so fast they hadn't even talked about it. He'd figured working closely together, she'd keep her maiden name so there was less confusion when people referred to them.

She said, "I'm an O'Connell."

Liam squeezed her neck, his face close to hers. "Yes, you are. So, let's go save some people." He headed for the door with her right behind him.

They found another couple and a group of three women who looked to be two sisters on the tourist train with their mother. One had glass in her arm. When the sister reached for it, Liam said, "Hold up!" Her hand jerked back. "Don't pull it out. Let the doctors do it. Okay?"

The women nodded. Their mom said, "Come on, girls. This handsome man can help us out."

Roxie chuckled. She assisted the woman with glass in her arm while Liam walked with the other two. He held them steady and followed Roxie. Liam's gaze snagged on the back of her shoulder. "Rox, you're bleeding."

She half glanced over her shoulder. "I thought I felt something."

"Is she your sweetheart?" the mother asked him.

Liam smiled, helping the woman step out of the train. "Yes, ma'am. She is." He walked them to the grass and heard sirens approach in the distance. Roxie came over and slid her arms around his waist, giving him a quick hug.

Before she stepped away, he said, "Hold up."

He shifted his head to the other side of hers, not letting her go. He didn't want to, but he also could look at her wound up close that way.

"Feels like a scratch."

"It's deep but not stitches-deep."

"Thanks." She squeezed his waist, then let go.

They stayed close but not touching. Roxie looked at the train that had exploded. "Bomb, sabotage, or accident?"

Liam shook his head. "I guess we'll find out."

"Or, you know, whoever is assigned to investigate." She eyed him. "Since technically, we're victims."

Liam made a face. She laughed, and said, "Yeah, I don't like that word either. But it's just a designation. It's not a *label*. And it doesn't mean either of us has been defeated."

"Good."

Roxie smiled, but it faded fast. "People died today. This cost lives."

And it was supposed to have been their restful, peaceful vacation. Now part of their time off would be spent making statements to local law enforcement or the California Bureau of Investigation. FBI. ATF. Someone would show up to investigate this, and it would be out of his and Roxie's hands.

That didn't mean he wasn't going to put it on the taskforce radar. After all, everyone knew they were renegades. Why not embrace it?

He patted his pockets. "I still have your phone."

She took it, looking at the screen. "Huh. There's a text from an unknown number."

"Is that unusual?" Maybe there were other agents from training whose numbers she hadn't saved to her contacts.

"It just says, 'That was fun.'" Her brows rose. "I hope that doesn't mean what I think it means."

Liam looked at the wrecked train. "I hope so, too."

SIX

"Thanks." Roxie accepted the water bottle from Liam and twisted off the top. Now that she was done helping people, and the emergency services workers had taken the injured to the closest hospital, the adrenaline had dissipated enough she could feel the sting on the back of her shoulder.

Whatever she'd landed on when the train exploded had dug into her skin. She rolled her shoulders now, wincing, and removed her denim jacket. She laid it on the ground beside her.

An ocean of first responders wandered around the grassy area between where she sat under a tree and the train wreckage. Liam moved among them, going over to a firefighter before she lost track of him. She watched people move in and out of the train cars. Climbing up on top of the side that now faced the blue sky.

Half a dozen birds flew overhead, and she took a second to watch them, catching a moment of peace in the middle of chaos. Taking a breath was a learned skill. She'd figured out in the Marine Corps pretty fast that she might only have a split second at times to center herself, but that moment could give her the relief she needed.

Liam strode back over, a small packet in one hand. Something in the other. "Lean forward."

She turned slightly and leaned with her elbows on her knees.

He shifted her shirt strap out of the way, and she felt something cool touch her skin. Roxie hissed. He gently applied whatever he'd brought over and then covered it with gauze, which he taped down. "Good?"

"Can you imagine if we even tried to have a full-blown wedding reception and a service?" She chuckled, but there wasn't much strength to it. "It would probably end in a disaster." She glanced over at him, grinning, and caught the look on his face.

Not humor.

"What?"

He shook his head and sat on the grass beside her, downing a water bottle while she watched. That wasn't supposed to be sexy, but after the kiss he'd given her when they'd regained consciousness? She should figure out how she was going to be able to focus working with him. That kiss had been crazy distracting.

There had to be a reason couples weren't supposed to work together in law enforcement, but even with the tug of togetherness, she still would rather be with him than somewhere else.

Trusting someone else to watch her back.

With all they'd been through, she couldn't even imagine leaving that up to other people.

A few months ago, they'd been at a church when it was clear there was a bomb inside. She'd escorted

Clare—her former boss at Vanguard, who'd been pregnant at the time—outside. Liam had trusted her with that detail while he and his friends took care of the explosive. That division of labor had been a good idea, but it didn't mean she'd liked the low-key worry until she saw him walk out of that church.

There had been a drive-by shooting that day where multiple cops were killed in the crowd outside the church not long after the bomb was defused. Roxie had taken down the shooter so other police officers could arrest him.

She pulled her phone out again. "Okay, let's take a look at this text now." They'd opted to give themselves a few moments to not get caught up in adrenaline. It had been long enough now, so she read it aloud again. "That was fun."

Liam pulled out his phone. The screen was shattered, the thing nearly bent in half. "I was thinking it felt odd in my pocket."

"Guess we need to hit the phone store and get you a replacement." They had friends who could get intel on the text and the number it had come from. She forwarded the information to Simon.

"Call Talia."

"Right." Their team could run the number also. Roxie didn't want to think that she'd hit her head, but she had blacked out so who knew? TBIs were nothing to mess around with. Roxie pulled up the number and handed the phone to Liam. "Here."

He put the call on speaker so she heard it ring as she leaned back against the tree and closed her eyes. Did she want to admit there might be a connection between the train explosion and whoever had sent her that ominous text? It could be nothing. Easily.

Simply. This could be a wrong number, someone's random comment sent to a friend, and she received it in error.

But the abusive relationship she'd been in, and then getting effectively stalked by her ex's brother, collided to make her nerve endings spark. From a text.

She wanted to throw her phone away and not go to the phone store to get a new one. Why couldn't hers be the one that broke?

Liam set his hand on her leg. She started and opened her eyes. Before either of them could speak, the call connected. "This better not be about work, Mrs. O'Connell. You're supposed to be on vacation."

Roxie said, "Does it count as work if you're on a train, and it explodes?"

Talia Matrice, NSA agent and Northwest Counter Terrorism Taskforce member, gasped. "Say *what*?"

"I figured it would be all over the news by now." Roxie leaned against Liam.

"You okay, girl? How are you doing?"

Roxie said, "We're all right, but a lot of people aren't."

Liam explained the situation with his phone and the text.

"Send me everything. I'll run it down. Don't y'all worry, Talia's got this."

Roxie smiled. "Thanks, T."

Liam sent the information, typing on the screen while he said, "Any new chatter, possibly about this not being an accident?"

She was glad he asked, because she also wanted to know if a federal agency would be the ones investigating. Maybe even the NTSB, given it was a train. Her mind spun at a hundred miles an hour, and she couldn't get her thoughts to settle. But she knew one thing.

Roxie wanted to work this case if it wasn't an accident.

"Nothing before or immediately after. I'm seeing reports now filtering through," Talia said. "No one has claimed responsibility, but I'll keep an eye on that and let you know."

"Any idea who might be assigned the scene?" Liam had an interesting note in his voice.

He wanted to work the case?

Roxie said nothing yet, but if he wanted to, then she could admit she also would like to know who was behind this. Whether it was connected to the text. If it was CBI or even a federal agency, they could keep tabs and get included in updates as part of the taskforce. Their group worked under Homeland Security now, so it wasn't a stretch that they needed to know the results of the investigation.

"I'll let you know about that, too." Talia's voice had an odd tone.

Roxie lifted her brows. "You have something on the text, T?"

"You're not gonna like it."

Liam said, "Give it a shot."

"The phone isn't one connected to any known commercial network. It's on an entirely different system I've been working to crack for a long time. Longer than I'd like. It's a side project I tackle a piece at a time in my free time, like a puzzle book or adult coloring."

Roxie hadn't ever done any of those things. She

didn't play games on her phone, either. If she needed to switch off, then she walked her dog. Or sat outside and drank coffee where she could see at least a piece of nature.

"There's an info sec specialist somewhere out there who created a bootleg internet-based phone network that's completely untraceable. Bad guys get a phone that is set up with the software for this communication network, and nothing they do can be traced. When they contact anyone on the regular commercial networks, it uses a phone number that's a spoof account."

"So there's no way to trace it?"

Talia said, "I'd have to have direct live access in order to get into the system. What I need is someone who isn't governed by the strictures that exist around me as a federal agent. Someone who can get me one of these phones."

Given Roxie had sent the text information to Simon at Vanguard, maybe she'd already found that kind of person for Talia. "I'm gonna send you a contact. Give him a call from your personal phone. He's a good kid, and if there's anyone who can breach this thing, it's him."

Liam squeezed her shin. "Good idea." He sent Simon's contact information to Talia, and she saw him read the fact she'd sent the text information to the twins, but he said nothing about it. Did they need to have a conversation about her friends? She didn't think he objected, but when he scrolled down and paused on the thread with Destiny Reed, so far down it was practically buried, he frowned.

"For now," Talia said, "go ahead and try calling the number. Let's see if we can get anything."

Roxie took the phone from Liam. "Do you need to stay on the line?"

"No, you can hang up with me. I've connected to your phone through our system that, if anyone asks, doesn't exist."

Roxie smiled.

"Keep him talking at least a couple of minutes. I'll see what I can get."

"Copy that." Roxie ended the call and looked at Liam. "Ready?"

"Keep it on speaker. I wanna hear what this person has to say." He didn't look happy, that cloudy expression on his face creating shadows in his gray-blue eyes. "We need intel."

"So we can go back to our vacation?"

"You know we're working this if it's on us that it happened."

Roxie frowned. "Even if we're connected, it wasn't our responsibility. There's no blood on our hands. At least, not from this."

Liam reached over and tapped the screen, making the call and putting it on speaker. Apparently, that particular discussion was over. But that didn't mean they were done talking about it.

The male who answered the phone did so chuckling.

Roxie straightened away from the tree. "I don't see anything funny about this."

"Then we'll have to agree to disagree, won't we?"

Who was it? Should she use Darwish's name so he knew she remembered who he was? Rather than let that slip too early, she said, "The people you killed and those you injured, and their families, also aren't amused."

He cleared his throat. "Casualties are inevitable. It's how history records all the great changes."

"What change are you looking for?"

"I'll be sure to draft a manifesto for the world to read."

Roxie said, "I doubt anyone will care what you have to say. They don't even know who you are."

"When I'm done, the *world* will know who I am."

"Yeah, but they probably still won't care." She didn't like this guy's voice. Every time he spoke, his tone reverberated in a way that caused a tremor in her and made Roxie lean into Liam a little harder. "So maybe don't worry about it, yeah? That way, more people don't have to die."

Liam's chest jerked. Like he wanted to laugh but was holding it back.

Now wasn't the time for that!

Roxie shook her head. "What do you say? How about we both go about our lives, and we leave everyone else in peace?" It was worth a try, at least. Still, this man needed to be arrested for what he'd done here today, so it wasn't like anyone in law enforcement would quit hunting him.

He chuckled again. "Walk away? My dear, I'm just getting started."

The call ended.

A second later, she got a text from Talia.

> I got nothing. Who is this guy?

SEVEN

Liam tucked the phone between his shoulder and cheek so he had both hands free to stir milk into his coffee. "How is Bob?"

His mom said, "Oh, fine. Fine. You know."

He did not, which was why he was asking his mom about her *boyfriend*. He shuddered even thinking that word. Sure, his dad had been gone a long time. His mom didn't need to be a lonely cop widow the rest of her life. Bob had been a cop years ago, and his daughter was an FBI agent. No one mentioned the man's past, though Bob freely talked about it. The people he worked with at Vanguard, including Roxie at one point, spoke highly of him.

Liam shouldn't worry, except for the fact this was his mother. And they were talking about her love life. "Great." He managed not to sound too much like he was choking.

"And the two of you are absolutely fine? No lingering effects?"

"We're good, Mom. Promise."

"Keep yourselves that way, okay?" She sounded worried still. Maybe the lingering fear from losing her husband, and then last year when Conrad had been attacked. Rory lived up in Alaska running the same restaurant Conrad ran in Benson. Two brothers, so alike, who refused to see the similarities between them.

"Only if you promise to keep praying."

His mother chuckled. "I am, honey. Don't worry about me. You have plenty to handle with that tough girl wrapped in a ball of gorgeous by your side."

Liam smiled to the refrigerator, put the milk away, and shut the door. "Yes, I do."

"Did you ask her?"

He had hoped she wouldn't follow up on the subject of their last conversation. His mom knew all about the ring—currently back on the chain with his dog tags around his neck. He'd told her he planned to ask Roxie. "She doesn't want to spend the money on something that will be a one-time event."

Which encompassed vacations, fun trips, and all parties, depending on how a person looked at it.

"And you think that's what it is?"

"What am I supposed to think?" He turned and leaned against the counter in the cabin they'd rented, able to see Roxie on the porch at the table. She sat forward on the chair, typing on her laptop. "That's what she said it was."

Still, they'd kind of been mid-conversation with nothing settled when the train exploded. Of all things, that hadn't been how he expected yesterday to go. So much for a quiet break away from their lives.

"Dig a little. It's just a service and a party. It doesn't have to be crazy extravagant, but your friends want to celebrate with you. There are going to be so many weddings this summer. You'll realize you never gave that gift to yourselves, being able to allow your friends to wish you congratulations. To celebrate what you've found with each other."

Liam frowned. "And if she doesn't want to?"

"Make sure it's a good reason, and not just because she's scared."

"I don't think she's afraid of getting married. We already did that."

"Just the two of you."

Was that it? She just didn't need to make a spectacle of it? Liam wasn't sure that was the reason he'd chalk it up to. He for one would quite like to celebrate with his friends and family. Roxie could invite her...

He lifted his chin and stared at her.

Apart from a half dozen friends, who would she invite? She didn't have family that he knew of, not anymore. Everyone she loved had died. She was terrified of something bad happening to their dog, Pronto. Probably to Liam as well, but he wasn't going to let that happen.

Lord, You're the one that takes care of that stuff. A woman who has lost so much shouldn't lose anything more.

Was that why she didn't want to have a big wedding celebration? Maybe she worried she wouldn't have *anyone* to invite. That if she had to walk down the aisle, she would be doing it alone. She hadn't wanted to do the aisle thing at the courthouse. They'd simply stood together. Just the two of them, not the disproportionate number of family they each had. One piece of paper, and she'd changed her professional name to be his last name.

That had to be it.

"I'll leave you to it. Love you, Lee."

"Love you, too, Mom." He stuck his phone in his pocket and took two cups of coffee outside to the table. He set Roxie's beside her laptop, his head still full of thoughts about weddings.

"Everything good?"

Liam nodded. He wanted to kiss her forehead, but he needed to keep his hands to himself, or they'd get no work done. He settled for pulling his chair close. "What are you working on, Marshal O'Connell?"

He had to admit, he liked that she wanted to take his name, not just personally but professionally also. Several of their friends who'd married, and teammates with the Northwest Counter Terrorism Taskforce, kept their names separate at work. Roxie claimed him for whoever cared to know.

"Nothing if you're gonna look at me like that."

He grinned over the rim of his coffee. "Then distract me with work talk."

She chuckled, then sighed. "The NTSB and the FBI are working the scene, but Peter said that Stella told him that her friend who works out of Oakland knows a guy on the team. The initial word is that there was no trace of components for an incendiary device found in the wreckage. That it's looking like they're going to officially rule it as an accident, maybe sabotage, but not a terrorist attack."

"That doesn't make sense when our friend on the phone said he did it for fun."

"Maybe that's what he meant. That it was sabotage meant to inconvenience us and hurt people. Not that it was an attack or a precursor to something else."

Liam said, "Something bigger? He did say he was just getting started."

She shrugged, sitting back in her chair with the mug in her hands. "If it's ruled an accident, there will be an investigation, but no one is going to be looking for a suspect."

"And if they did, it wouldn't be for a guy the government declared dead years ago." Liam wanted someone to investigate, and if that had to be him and Roxie on their week off, then so be it. But it wasn't exactly his preference when the alternative was a candlelight dinner and nothing to do but stare at the stars.

He sipped his coffee and stared at the hill that dropped off just after the porch. The rolling grassy landscape swept and flowed down to the valley, dotted with trees. Between two, he spotted sprawling rows of grape vines. "This is a nice place."

"We should come back on our anniversary, like make it a regular thing."

Liam glanced over and watched her look at the landscape the way he had. "As long as we're not thinking about exploding trains, scratches, and bruises while we're here."

"Or supposedly dead generals."

Liam said, "I can if you can."

"Oh, it's like that is it?" She grinned. "Fine. We just have to finish this out, then it's nothing but blue skies and not a care in the world."

That sounded kind of amazing. It had also been the intention for them coming here to switch off and spend time together.

Evidently, she wasn't even going to let a threat spoil her week.

He heard a vibration and lifted her phone to find a movement alert on Pronto's crate. "How is she?"

"Still confined to the crate for hours so she'll rest, which she does *not* like, according to Dakota. They're doing some training that doesn't involve much movement, but which exercises her brain, which is perfect."

"Dakota knows what she's doing with a working dog."

Roxie nodded. "She also called her previous boss, Victoria Bramlyn, who has connections with the CIA. She sent over an email after Victoria made some calls. Apparently, the CIA considers General Darwish to be dead. However, they had a CIA officer a few years ago who sat in a meeting and reported back that someone who looked a whole lot like Darwish was in the room. The officer was killed a few weeks later, so no one ever followed up on it. The intel slipped through the cracks in favor of the officer's actual mission and his death."

"The government isn't going to search for a dead man. If we're going to convince them Darwish is still alive, we'll need proof." Which meant they'd have to get up close and personal. A photo, or video, and DNA that could be tested, not just whatever airport security could find.

Roxie said, "Even that will have to be scrutinized. No one wants to look like they made a mistake, so we'll still get pushback no matter what."

"Maybe that CIA guy left something useful in his report." Liam didn't like spies, mostly because the ones he'd met strutted around like they owned everything. And they wanted to do it all solo.

He much preferred a fire team who sweat, bled,

and fought side-by-side, watching each other's backs. That was the relationship he and Roxie had always had. It had been necessary that was all they were to each other in the Marines. Things were different now, sure. Getting married couldn't help flexing what was between them into a whole new sphere.

He tipped his head. "Do you want kids...like, at some point?"

Roxie blinked. "Sure. Doesn't everyone?"

"I don't think so." He shrugged. "Some people, single or couples, are happy being child free. Just because we're married doesn't mean we have to have kids. I just want us to be content with whatever we choose."

She studied the horizon again, quiet for a minute or so before she said, "I'd prefer contentment to regret, or thinking I missed something I should've grabbed hold of."

"Me, too. That's why I'm asking while it's not really the right time."

"That makes me wonder if it will ever feel like it's the 'right time.'"

He could concede that. "True. It's okay for us to settle. Work together for a while. Find a rhythm. If we come back here on our anniversary every year, we can revisit the conversation. Discuss what the next year is going to hold."

She sent him a soft smile. "It's a date."

Liam leaned over toward her. "Yeah?"

She rolled her eyes but touched her lips to his. "Yeah, hero. You tell me when, and I'll toss my birth control in the trash. Just for you."

Those last three words had a note of something else in them. She wasn't being entirely light with this.

Her history might've given her a boundary with discussions of pregnancy. She probably never intended to bring a child into the situation with Mark Mills, too fearful that the baby would not only tie her to him forever but also give him yet more leverage to hurt both of them.

Liam wanted forever.

He wanted to be connected to Roxie every way they could be, so long as she freely entered into it. Not because he'd pressured her or acted like a man who had terrorized her for years until she escaped.

He wanted a child with her nose and those eyes. A son he could tell stories about his father to, that he could teach to be the protector the way his dad had taught him. A girl who would be as tough and as soft as Roxie. Cousins for Conrad's kids, and grandchildren for his mom to spoil.

He leaned over again, gently taking hold of her chin. "It's a date."

Warmth and that contentment he always wanted her to have shone in her eyes. Zero fear.

And that was the way he wanted it to stay.

EIGHT

"We should at least run."
Beside her, Liam shook his head. "Nope. We're *strolling*. Do you know what that word means?"

Roxie had a sneaking suspicion she didn't. It turned out she was in the right line of work, but how did that help with the time she was supposed to switch off and couldn't seem to? Or didn't know how. She let go of a long sigh.

Liam chuckled, snagging her hand so he could hold it while they walked down this single lane country road that made up the perimeter of the property. Eight cabins, though only two or three looked occupied if cars out front were anything to go by. "Tell me what you're thinking about."

"That barn smelled." She was terrible at this. At least when she walked Pronto, she could focus on the dog rather than the nothing happening around her. "And I have an email in my inbox from the local US Marshal office, the one closest to our work. He wants me to come in so he can meet the 'liaison' between them and 'the feds,' as he put it. I'm supposed to report first thing Monday."

"It's not always easy to have to work both sides."

She shrugged. "It was the agreement. I'm part of the taskforce because they had an open spot, and it's a marshal who fills that chair. So, I became a marshal."

"Just like that."

Did he want her to shrug again?

"Most people have to work at it more than that. Or it's a dream they have for years. For you, it seems more like a means to an end."

"Well, they let me throw guys to the ground."

"Hopefully just bad guys." He grinned.

"Depends how you play your cards."

Liam laughed aloud.

She returned it with a smile of her own. "I know some people dream of the life I have. I know that."

"I didn't mean you're ungrateful. I meant you have the potential to accomplish things some people work for years to reach a point where they're able to even qualify."

"They didn't have years with an O'Connell as their squad sergeant, teaching them how to be amazing. I did. You think I didn't work for it?" She'd practically killed herself giving everything she had to make sure he knew he could count on her.

"So it's just about me."

"Uh, duh. Only ever." She rolled her eyes.

"So romantic."

"That's me. Queen of romance. It's why I'm a man hunter now. Dragging fugitives back to jail and looking good doing it."

Liam had to stop walking he was laughing so hard, something she didn't think she'd ever seen him do. It went on long enough she could pull out her phone and slide her thumb up the screen. She snapped a photo of him, but he saw it and tried to wrestle the phone from her.

"You wouldn't dare."

She wrapped her arms around his neck and kissed him, which put the phone out of reach behind his head. Things were starting to get interesting when she felt something at the edge of her senses. Since she'd honed her instincts in live fire battle situations, she pulled back just far enough she could slide her nose along the side of his. "Someone is watching us."

He rubbed one hand up and down her back, avoiding the bandage he'd replaced this morning, his other arm around her waist holding her close to him. "Your three o'clock?"

She nodded.

"Are you armed?"

She had on skinny jeans and a fitted T-shirt. "Where would I have hidden a gun?" They were supposed to be on vacation. She wasn't going to walk around with a gun within reach so she could react every time she was afraid.

"Doesn't mean you're not armed." He eyed her in that knowing way.

"Fine." She huffed. "Two knives, one in each boot."

"That's my girl." He grinned, and she could've fainted at the look in his eyes if this was the Victorian era or she had some kind of lung problem. "Front of my belt, my right side. So we're good if we need it."

His gun was out of view of their three o'clock. If she wanted to, she could slide her hand down his chest and find the gun. But sliding it from the holster on his belt meant disarming him just so she could feel more reassured. Something Liam O'Connell would absolutely let her do. He was the kind of guy who allowed himself to be vulnerable just so she could feel strong.

"They haven't moved. They're just watching us."

"Let's go back. Not a stretch that we might want to hurry back to the cabin. What with us being newlyweds and all."

"Except the fact we're armed and dangerous." He still kept the gun out of sight. Turning away from whoever was in the trees, she made a quick scan of their surroundings.

"Just means they'll know we're not dumb."

They walked together back toward the cabin. It was just after lunch so the sun remained high in the sky. No sound of freeway traffic or the sirens that came with a city at all hours of the day and night. She had spent more time in urban areas than nearly anywhere else, aside from the desert of the middle east. Nature wasn't something she sought out, but she could see the appeal out here in the quiet.

It was so...still.

Which honestly made it easier to sense when something was amiss. Like the fact there was more than one person out here. Hiding. Behind a tree—or in one. Behind that tractor. Or in the barn to their right. Tracking them as they made progress up the lane back to the cabin.

His phone ringing startled her.

Liam looked at his watch. "It's Dakota."

"You should answer it." She could watch their backs while he talked on the phone. After all, the gun was on her side of his belt, so she'd be able to grab it easily in a split second. "Find out what she needs to tell you."

Liam picked up his pace. He held the phone to his ear. "O'Connell." He paused. "Yeah, she is. I'll relay whatever it is."

Roxie looked at the barn again. There was absolutely someone in the shadows. Her steps faltered even though she wanted to appear strong. Liam wrapped an arm around her neck, tugging her to his side while he spoke to their boss.

She looked again at the barn but saw nothing.

Whoever was following, it wasn't about ambushing them or attacking. It was purely observation. *Interesting.* Who would come this close while they were effectively on their honeymoon and just watch? The idea was pretty creepy, to say the least. They'd have to make sure they closed all the blinds in the cabin even if that meant they couldn't see a threat coming.

"Thanks, boss." He hung up just as they got to the edge of the cabin property. "I'll tell you inside."

Roxie closed the door right behind them, locking it immediately. They'd left the door unlocked when they went out, so now she checked the doors and windows. When they stood together, she glanced at the closest window, then touched Liam's arms and shifted him to the left a little. "Right there. Then they can't see you."

He glanced at the window but didn't move. "Who?"

"Whoever was watching outside." She quickly said, "What did Dakota tell you?"

"Apparently, there's a Chinese national, a CEO high up in their banking world, and he's set to visit the US in a couple of days. He'll be going to San Francisco, visiting Silicon Valley and all the big tech firms there, and then going to Los Angeles for dinner with the Chinese Ambassador and a movie premier."

"That's the only local thing?" Darwish had to want something, or why be in that airport? When Liam nodded, she said, "Did they change his destination airport?"

"He was never set to come into the same one we landed at. So, unless it was Darwish arriving the day we saw him, then I have no idea why he'd be up in Washington."

Roxie had no clue either, unfortunately. "But he's down here now, or he's working down here. Could be there are people locally operating on his behalf, and he's nowhere near this area."

How did they find out if Darwish had a score to settle with the Chinese businessman, or if the guy had threats against him?

Liam said, "There's a group on the web Talia found. They want to destabilize the biggest world economies. The end goal is war between Russia, the US, China, and Europe, basically pitting us all against each other."

"And killing this guy could kick off something serious." Wars had been started on a lot less.

Liam nodded. "Dakota is going to have Homeland Security contact him so his security team is fully briefed. But right now, there's only speculation, no concrete threats."

But this guy was the most likely candidate.

"Now tell me who is outside."

"If I knew, I would." Roxie folded her arms, tapping her foot on the entryway tile. "I didn't see a face."

If it was dark, she would head out with a gun and take a look for herself. Do some sneaking of her own, see what she could find. Too bad it was daylight outside.

"Anything from Dakota about Darwish?" She'd quite like to sneak around where he was in the dark. Put some of her fresh US Marshal training to good use and bring in a dangerous fugitive. Prove to everyone that somehow he'd bested their squad the first time, but America never let that happen twice.

That didn't sit right, but it just made this a score they had to settle. After all, they'd found out they had most likely been duped. Lied to. They'd wrongly believed the mission to be complete and now it was up to them to set things right.

Lord, help us set it right.

She looked at her phone but other than another movement notification she had for Pronto's crate—when the dog got up and turned around before lying back down again—she had nothing. No calls or texts. No family messages or personal emails.

Liam was here. Who else would be contacting her? "Have you spoken to Destiny much since she got home?"

"Oh, uh. Not really." She had left a couple of voicemails, but Destiny never returned them. Now she knew from Liam who'd heard from Blake that her friend was pregnant. Roxie had cried over the kidnapping in a foreign country that had led to Destiny being in that condition. "It's fine. She's got things going on."

She just had to be content with what she had

here. With this new relationship with Liam. She didn't need to slow down so much that all the...lack hit her like a truck. Or like an explosion.

She strode into the living room. "I'm going to pull the drapes. Just in case."

So what if she had to clear her throat a couple of times. Why did he have to bring up Destiny? They'd been roommates for a few weeks, but apparently that was it as far as Destiny was concerned. Roxie had made a couple of friends in Marshals training. It wasn't going to go anywhere, so why put much effort into it? Between her best girl, Pronto, and all that she gained with Liam—marriage and a new purpose in her career—what else did she need or have time for?

Roxie sniffed, settling the curtains together over the front window. At the end of the yard, beside the check-in building, she spotted a lone figure. Close enough she could make out some of his features.

Speaking of lack...

She had to be having some kind of mental breakdown. After all, why else would she be seeing her dead brother outside, years after he'd been killed in action.

She needed to get back to work, or she was going to lose it.

NINE

Liam blinked against the darkness, letting his body and mind wake up while he catalogued what had woken him up. A sound? The sense of someone in the cabin? The red digital clock readout said 02:14.

The tangy wood smell of smoke hit his senses.

Liam sat up, pushing back the covers as he went. Years of being woken up for police work had him reaching for his clothes. Something was definitely wrong. He could see a glow between the window blinds...and under the bedroom door. He reached for the lamp and flicked it on rather than shaking Roxie awake.

"Get up, Helton!" He barked it like an order, not loving the fact he couldn't softly ease her from sleep. He had to fall back on that Marine training.

She was up and reaching for her clothes in seconds. "What's going on?" There was a split-second pause, and she said, "Why does it smell like smoke?"

"Let's find out. Put your boots on." He slid the holstered gun onto his belt and grabbed his T-shirt, toeing his boots on but not lacing them up yet.

He opened the bedroom door to flames across the room. The kitchen had been fully engulfed, the window shattered. Broken glass across the floor.

"Fire extinguisher?" She started to move past him.

Liam snagged her arm just as the gas in the stove gave a whoosh. "Run." He tugged her arm to the front door and got it open just as the force slammed into them.

He hit the concrete pavers of the front walk. Roxie landed on his leg, and partially on the grass. He scrambled out from under her and hauled her up. "Come on."

The roof collapsed, more of the cabin swallowed up by flames. He had friends who were firefighters, and he had assisted in traffic accidents where the cars were on fire but had no desire to try and fight a blaze. Not when the person who smashed out that window and set the cabin ablaze—he was thinking it had probably been a Molotov cocktail—was likely still out here.

"Split up or stick together?"

Roxie drew her weapon from the holster on her belt. "You go left, I'll go right, circle around the house."

"Copy that." He scanned around him, circling their cabin. Someone else stood on their porch. Liam called out, "Call 911."

"Already did, bro," the guy called out. "Why do you have a gun? Are you a cop?"

"Yes. Go back inside." He continued around the back of the cabin, watching for someone lurking. Or even footsteps that might indicate where the perpetrator had gone. He moved swiftly and met Roxie at the back.

"There." She motioned toward the road behind the cabin and a break in the wood fence, then took off running.

Liam chased her, more than chasing down whatever—and whoever—she had seen.

Roxie ducked down and scrambled under the fence, where two tall slats had been broken away. Had it been this way earlier or when they first arrived? Someone could easily have snuck up close to the cabin this way, intent on causing havoc.

Liam's shoulders caught on one side. He pushed through, dragging the outside of his arm across the splintered end of the wood. He hissed against it and did the hard thing anyway, rushing after his wife just as she jump-tackled a guy.

The second man, standing beside a pickup truck, aimed his gun. Liam squeezed off two shots, and the man dropped to the ground. He glanced once at Roxie and saw she was good for a second at least, then ran to the guy he'd shot. Liam kicked the gun away from his hand, but the guy was dead.

No one else. Just these two.

He went back to Roxie, hearing sirens approach from the west. The man she'd tackled swept her onto her back. Liam held aim on the guy. "Let her go, back up, and stand up. I wanna see your hands the whole time." He poured all the years of police arrests into his tone but not consciously. More like a switch flipped in him, and it just initiated on its own.

The guy froze for a second, then Liam caught the flash of a knife blade in the dark. A wicked shimmer of metal swung out, launching off Roxie toward him.

Liam squeezed off another two shots.

The guy hit the ground, and the knife clattered on stone.

Liam let out a frustrated sound.

"Why are you mad?" Roxie held out her hand, and he assisted her off the ground. "You did the right thing."

"It's considerably harder to question someone who is dead."

She let out a huff of amusement a lot like a heavy breath from the exertion. "I guess that's true. But we can figure out who they were."

A fire truck pulled into the complex main entrance.

"We need local PD here." Because while it was Liam's case, assuming the bombing and this event were connected, the local law enforcement officers were the ones who were going to oversee the two dead guys. He bent forward and gave himself a second to suck in a couple of breaths.

When he straightened, Roxie was looking around, a note in her body language that looked a lot like hours ago after their walk. As if she'd seen something. He said, "Tell me what it is." Not a command, but more of an invitation for her to share.

"Nothing." She shook her head. "It can't be anything, just me needing more sleep."

That wasn't going to happen tonight.

"Thanks for saving me."

He pulled her close. "Always. Forever."

"Don't get a cheesy song stuck in my head." She sighed. "We should search these guys for ID."

"You check the truck. I'll look for wallets." They

would be disturbing the scene, but they also knew how to do that minimally.

A firefighter peered over the fence. "You guys staying out of the way of the fire?"

"It's our cabin," Liam called back. "And I'm guessing these guys set the fire, so we're gonna need police officers."

"I'll radio it in, but I think there's a unit inbound."

"Thanks."

"You guys cops?" The guy probably knew the look—and the mannerisms—of officers.

"Feds."

He lifted his chin. "Stay there."

Liam bent to the knife-guy and patted front and back pants pockets, not moving the guy too much. He found a wallet in the guy's back left pocket. When he pulled it out, he took a photo and used the taskforce secure messaging app to send the image to the team. Crandall Hooper's driver's license was local, and he was forty-two. Liam returned the wallet where he'd found it.

He found a phone along with a tiny amount of narcotics in plastic wrap in the inside jacket pocket. "This might be one of those secure network phones." The police would be taking all this into evidence, but he still wanted the intel before they processed it.

Roxie wandered over. "Truck is registered to Bill Sears out of Monterey."

"That's hours from here. It was probably stolen, but we can look it up." These two might have taken it from a local, or they might've driven it up from central California.

"Cops are here."

He nodded. "Good."

The black and white vehicle pulled up on the main street that ran perpendicular to the one they were on. People had gathered around the cabin in the resort complex, but on this side of the fence, Liam only spotted a light on in someone's bedroom window.

He turned on the flashlight on his phone and waved at the cop. The male officer who came over had short dark hair and a scar on the side of his neck above the collar of his uniform shirt. He walked like it had been a long night, but the chance to work energized him.

Liam knew well how that felt. "Homeland Security. We're with an inter-agency taskforce, so I'll come back as a police sergeant from Washington State when you run my name."

"Got it. ID?"

"In the cabin." Liam motioned to the flickering wreckage the firefighters were now spraying water on. He holstered his weapon. As soon as they were done, and the place was clear, he wanted to get back in and find the metal part of his badge. Get it cleaned off so he could take it with him, even if he didn't have his ID.

Roxie said, "We chased these two from the house." Her tone almost sounded sad.

"You a cop, too?" the officer asked.

"US Marshal."

"And your badge is in the cabin as well?" It wasn't that he thought they were lying. It was that he'd have to account for what he knew and wanted all the information.

"Actually, I have a copy of my ID on my phone." She showed him the screen, her gun on her hip now. Her photo and credentials illuminated. "I took a photo of it just in case."

"Good thing." The cop nodded. "I'll call my supervisor and get the coroner out here. You'll both have to give statements. How long are you in the area?"

Liam said, "A few more—"

Roxie cut him off. "Until this is done."

The cop glanced between them. "Got it. Stay close but out of the way."

Liam snagged his wife's hand, and they stepped over toward the fence while the officer got on his radio, talking as he circled the bodies and the truck. Out of the man's earshot, he spoke low asking Roxie, "Who were you looking for? When you were looking around?"

She frowned. "I just didn't want there to be anyone else around that I missed. There were more than two people around us yesterday when we were walking, so did they leave, or did only two stay here to try and kill us?"

If someone wanted them dead, Liam figured they'd have to try a lot harder than igniting the kitchen. "They didn't mean us harm yesterday, or they'd have tried to hurt us then. It seemed more like observing us."

"Yeah, getting information so they could do this." She swung her hand out toward the cabin.

Liam wasn't so sure. "It didn't seem malicious."

"And you can tell that by someone watching you?"

"Kind of, honestly. It's instinct, and I didn't get that sense."

Roxie frowned, watching the firefighters work on the cabin over the fence. Not looking at the dead bodies. On purpose because she didn't want some trauma to flip a switch and mess with her head? Or was it because their vacation was currently going up in flames?

"Someone ordered these guys to do this." Liam gently squeezed the tendon where her neck met her shoulder, then left his hand there. She leaned into him in that way she did, seeking solace from his nearness. *Lord, keep us safe.*

Their lives were inherently dangerous, but they'd survived to this point. Safety wasn't an illusion, and it wasn't the ultimate goal. It was more like a means to an end so they could do what they'd been put on this earth to do—and watch each other's backs through it.

"We need to touch base with the team."

Liam said, "My laptop is still in the car. We can look up what we have. Find out who these guys are, and who they're affiliated with."

She nodded, squeezing his hip. Despite the reassurance, he still got the feeling she was waiting for something else to happen. A shoe to drop, so to speak. He didn't think she'd lied to him, but she may have withheld truth that wasn't relevant to what was going on.

He couldn't help feeling like she kept parts of herself behind a wall. Maybe it would take a lifetime of discovery, or years where she would incrementally come to trust him. Liam wasn't going to demand that she suddenly become all-in. He just happened to be a lot simpler in the way he was wired. Roxie was the most complex woman he'd ever met, and it was a pleasure to show her every day that she could keep leaning on him.

But the question remained. Something was happening here that she wasn't saying.

Was she going to let him in?

TEN

"You want us to what?"

Roxie gripped the phone with one hand, the edge of the sink with the other, trying to keep her voice low in the single occupancy bathroom of the coffee shop. They'd come into town in the car after spending hours with the police and then getting breakfast. They'd hit a store and bought a few changes of clothes, along with a small suitcase each to put their things in.

Nearly everything had gone up in flames, and what didn't smelled like smoke.

"Simon can find a photo of him, right? The military has to have one." The twins had her on speaker. "Adam Russell Helton." She rattled off his date of birth, his Army company, and a few other things she could think of.

"Why do I need to find him?"

Sometimes on the phone, she couldn't tell the twins apart, even though in person, they were very different. Peter had opted to become an operator for Vanguard while Simon worked in their tech department—sometimes it seemed like he *was* the tech department.

Still, she knew that question had come from Simon as soon as she heard Peter's tone when he said, "Bro, isn't it obvious she wants to know what happened?"

"Yeah, but why now?"

Roxie said, "I think I saw him. It's crazy because he's been dead for years."

"But you saw another supposedly dead guy the other day."

No one pointed out the fact this was probably only her mind playing tricks on her. Wishing for something she couldn't have because this impossibility had happened. So why not?

There was no way her brother Adam was alive. He'd been killed while serving in the army, and they had buried him. *Case closed*. Why worry about it? She had plenty to occupy her right now, but there had been someone watching them the other day—multiple someones in fact.

"We should talk about the fact your cabin burned down."

Roxie said, "What is there to talk about? We're finding another place to stay, and the Northwest Counter Terrorism Taskforce is on the case."

"But you want us on this?" Peter's tone had softened.

Roxie stared at the sink rather than looking at her bedraggled self in the mirror. "Yes, please."

"Anything. You know that."

She swallowed against the lump in her throat. "Thanks."

Roxie hung up before they could ask her how she

was doing. The cabin had burned down, Liam had shot two guys, and they were waiting to find out who the men were. She was mainlining coffee, needed a shower, and planned to take a nap later wherever they booked to stay the next few nights.

Things hadn't exactly spun out of control, but she was having trouble hanging on, regardless.

So much for returning to work after a week off to relax. They were going to need a vacation from their vacation after this was done.

She splashed water on her face and went out to find Liam. He spotted her coming like a radar attuned only to her frequency, except that the guy had crazy instincts in situational awareness. She said, "Got something?"

He lifted his chin and motioned to a fresh white paper cup with a lid on her side of the table. "Another latte and an answer on the IDs."

She slid into the hard wood chair. "Both men?"

He nodded, then turned the laptop so she could see. "The guy by the truck had a fake driver's license, but his fingerprints came back as a dead guy."

Her eyebrows rose. "And his friend with the knife?"

Liam said, "Him, too. Both of them were civilian contractors about ten years ago. There was an attack at the base where they were working, and both were said to have been killed in a missile strike."

"Anywhere near where we were?"

He shook his head. "I heard about it, but we were hours away."

Roxie sipped her coffee while he told her more about the company the two men were attached to, and the work they were doing overseas before their supposed deaths. Now it was more important than it had been before that she find out if her brother hadn't been killed.

"Rox? You listening?"

Uh... "Why are dead people running around trying to kill people and blowing up trains? This has to be what Darwish meant when he said he was just getting started."

"But we have no idea where he is. Everyone we can ask for a favor in the federal community is keeping an eye out for the guy so we can prove he's alive."

"And now these guys?" She waved at the screen and a drip of coffee sloshed onto her thumb. She set the cup down and wiped it with a napkin. "Something is going on."

"My guess? They work for Darwish, and he paid them to hit our cabin with a Molotov cocktail." His gray eyes darkened.

She needed a lead to track down Darwish. A way to find him or to figure out what he was planning beyond speculation about a Chinese banker. "Anything from their phones?"

"I'm glad you asked." He winked at her. "They are connected to the number that messaged you, which you called. Their phones aren't on the secure network, though."

"Maybe they didn't rank high enough to warrant special untraceable phones."

He nodded, typing swiftly on the laptop keyboard. "I agree. From the communications, we can see there was some kind of request made and confirmation of it being done a few moments before we woke up to the fire."

"Anything about a wider plan?" She scanned the text conversation on the screen. "Like there." It looked like gibberish code to her, but most bad guys didn't type out criminal dealings in plain text for all the world—and the police—to be able to read. A lot of it was a shorthand code, or even emojis that stood for things.

"Talia has all of this. If there's a code, she'll figure it out. But from the numbering right here"—he pointed to a spot with a 1, 2, and a 3 written like a list. Next to each number was an emoji of fruit, a method of transport, and a series of Roman numerals—"we might be able to go so far as to guess three separate events."

"Like attacks?" She studied them. "And this is place and time, or a person and what they're doing?"

"Talia will run some scenarios, and we can take a look at what fits and makes the most sense."

She didn't want to be frustrated, or she would end up being like this for every case they worked. Who knew police work was a whole lot of questions and not much in the way of answers? Criminals who worked across state lines, across countries, and dealt death on a mass scale were either excellent at covering their tracks and staying out of the eagle eye of law enforcement, or they were dead because they'd enacted their plan, and in order to ensure success, had sacrificed themselves. She tried not to begrudge anyone their personal beliefs, but if a person was going to lay down their life, then why not do it for justice? For good.

Not for evil.

But then, that was probably what separated cops from fundamentalist martyrs. Both sides believed strongly enough to be willing to lay down their lives. But while one group wanted to destroy the enemy, her side only sought justice—not murder.

Liam set his coffee down. "There's evidence in the military reports we were able to access that our two cabin burning friends were under suspicion that they might've been trafficking drugs from the Middle East on military transports and using drug mules back to the US."

"So not good guys. Which makes this not a stretch." But faking their deaths, or sneaking away knowing they'd be declared dead so they could go on with their crimes? "Except the conspiracy part where we now have multiple people dead and yet walking around?"

An older man in a suit walked by them, holding a leather folder. He glanced at them with an odd expression.

Liam didn't seem bothered by it, so she didn't worry. Or, at least, tried not to. Just because someone had overheard them didn't mean a breach of security, and it didn't mean they were being watched every second.

So what if Darwish had found them?

If he was having fun, messing with them.

Roxie rolled her shoulders. It wasn't personal. She hadn't seen her brother. It had simply been her mind playing tricks on her. After all, it would be far too much of a coincidence if he really had shown up here. Now. In the middle of all this.

Probably all that happened was that her mind wanted to find something good. Before she even realized it, her brain had assimilated the concept of someone back from the dead and tried to create what she might've wished for.

Someone to walk her down the aisle.

"Hungry?"

Roxie stared out the window. She shook her head. "You?"

"Yes. I need a burrito, and you need some queso dip."

Well, she didn't exactly have to be hungry for that. It was cheese. "Let's feed you then." She checked her phone and saw nothing from Simon and Peter. There were a couple of texts from Dakota about Pronto, who'd been for a short walk this morning and tried to chase a squirrel.

Liam stepped out first, and she followed him to the car. She couldn't shake the tension and wasn't sure anyone would blame her for having it. Liam said something, but her ears didn't want to assimilate the sound. She just shook her head and slid in the front seat while he held the door for her.

Roxie leaned her head back and closed her eyes, trying to pray through what she was feeling. Exhaustion. Confusion. Her mind chose that moment to remind her that her birth control had burned in the cabin along with everything else, except his badge and her Marshal star.

It felt like a mental face-palm. Another thing she needed to worry about. Who had time for scary guys when there were day-to-day essentials to take care of?

She was getting a crash course in work/life balance, that was for sure.

Roxie reached back and slid out the laptop. She wanted to stare some more at that one, two, three code. Not that she thought she'd be able to crack the code before an NSA officer did. Federal law enforcement had databases of codes and algorithms. Ways to decipher even the most complex hidden messages.

She stared at the fruit, then the transportation. "A train, a plane, and a boat."

"What are you thinkin', Rox?" Liam's forearms flexed, but she wasn't going to get distracted by him driving.

"A depot, an airport, and a port? Or something comes in by boat, gets loaded on a train, and heads to the airport?" No, that didn't make sense. What would go that route? "Three attacks?"

"If it is, it would have a huge impact. The response alone would create chaos for just one of those."

"A train with a bomb, a plane with a bomb, and a boat with one?" They'd already encountered the first. "Maybe the first one already happened. We were there. Next will be a plane, is that it?"

"I hope not."

Roxie winced. "Whatever it is, I think we need to pray. And hope someone figures it out before something terrible happens."

People had already died. Things could very well already be set in motion, but she had to remind herself that law enforcement foiled terror plots on a regular basis that most people never even knew about. They simply carried on with their lives unaware.

She wanted that outcome, rather than the worst-case scenarios rolling through her mind.

How did they stop Darwish?

ELEVEN

Liam closed the bedroom door and stepped softly back to the coffee pot in the suite he had booked for them. Considerably pricier than the cabin, but far easier to defend. No one could climb up the exterior wall to the fourth floor, and there were still two floors above them, so no rappelling down either.

The hall had recently been renovated, so those signs on the walls were missing, and they'd circled the floor twice before figuring out what corner their room was tucked in—close to the emergency exit stairs, to which Liam had added a camera with a motion sensor he'd picked up while Roxie had chosen her clothes.

He reached for his phone on the coffee table, realized that was hers, and grabbed his instead. He'd already used her cell to try and contact Darwish. What else was there to do? They needed a lead.

Roxie was still asleep, but then, it was nearly five in the morning. She would see the call he'd tried to make when she looked. Hopefully, she wouldn't begrudge him the need to do *something*.

He called the office.

"Northwest Counter—oh, hey bro." Special Agent Niall O'Caran, NCIS, had been part of the taskforce for several years now. As a federal agent for the Navy, he wasn't so far removed from the Marine Corps, at least in his experience of military life. He got it.

"Hey. Anything new?"

"I was just looking at something that came in half an hour ago."

Which meant he'd have called as soon as he had information to pass on. "Anything I should know?"

"At this time of the morning? You should be sleeping, which I would be if I wasn't on call tonight."

Sure, the guy would be home with his wife—one of their civilian employees—and their two kids. "Sorry."

"Actually, Finn has a nasty cough so I'm kind of staying away so I don't catch it." Niall chuckled. "Don't tell Haley."

"Your secret is safe with me."

"Uh oh," Niall said, still chuckling. "What are you hiding?"

"Nothing. Roxie isn't going to have a problem with it." She understood how he was wired because she happened to be wired the same way. They'd been Marines. Of course they would do what it took to protect each other.

"Sounds like you're trying to convince yourself."

Liam went over to the window, pulled back the edge of the blind, and peered at the parking lot. There might have been multiple someones watching them the other day, but no one was out there now.

They were safe up here. "I tried calling Darwish back on Roxie's phone. He didn't answer."

"Maybe he's busy."

"That's what I'm afraid of." Liam scrubbed a hand over the hair on the back of his head. He needed to get it cut given how long it had gotten while Roxie was gone. Then again, with her reaction when they saw each other at the airport, maybe he would leave it long. "Especially if the train explosion was the first of three, and Roxie and I are targets."

"Stay away from planes or boats for a while, yeah?"

Solid advice, but it didn't make him feel better. "Good idea." His tone came out pretty sardonic, but Niall was a big boy who could handle it.

"Low level guys like the two you killed? That could just be a distraction. Or their tasks, including the train, were to try and kill us. They couldn't finish the job when you shot them both."

That would be good. "But that means Darwish is doing something different, and we have no leads on what it is." Liam wasn't sure about the whole Chinese banker thing. But he also had no better ideas.

He rubbed a hand over his chest. This would be a good time to sit with his Bible, since he wasn't sleeping, and he could keep an eye out, plus also reconnect. Get a fresh perspective and let go of some of the tension tying his chest up like there were steel bands wrapped around his torso.

"Which brings me to this intel."

"Yeah?" Liam paced the living area of the suite to retrieve the coffee that had finished brewing.

"Homeland Security got copies of everything the

police gathered initially from the two men you killed."

"They burned down the cabin and tried to kill us." Then one had come at Liam with a knife, the other with a gun. Now he was tired *and* cranky.

Niall said, "The fake IDs they had driver's licenses for lived local to the area where you are, so I'm thinking they're hired guns these days. Mercenaries or whatnot, out to make a few bucks. One of them had a couple of different social media accounts under his fake name and plenty of pictures of him at a local dive bar. I guess he's a fan of karaoke night."

Liam squeezed the bridge of his nose. They could pay the dive bar a visit, but how might that help? "What about a home address?"

"Nada. But we also have reports coming in. Chatter the CIA has been picking up about a group of 'ghosts' who are made up of ex-officers of theirs supposedly killed in random accidents back home. Stuff no one would consider anything but a tragic accident. Then there are soldiers, special forces guys. Either KIA or their lives ended domestically in some—"

Liam finished for him. "Tragic accident? Is this anything more than rumors?"

Niall said, "Over at Langley, they call it *intel*."

Liam sipped his coffee and kept his mouth shut about that. After he'd thought for a second, he said, "If it's just a rumor, how do they know who makes up the group? Or if they're even good or bad."

"That's where their *intel* gets into a gray area. They're never gonna admit they know someone who betrayed them and defected to this group for hire. Or it's some kind of disgruntled terror cell made up of *our* people determined to cause chaos. You're right, we don't even know whose side they're on."

Liam said, "Who mentioned the Chinese banker first?"

"Now you're thinking like a fed."

"So, the CIA knows this group is out there, they know at least one person who is part of it—if not more. And they know who the target is. That's what I'm getting?"

Niall said, "How Darwish fits in, we don't know. Unless someone in the group is sympathetic to him. Could be he's the one in charge, and they're all followers." The NCIS agent grunted. "But maybe a fed isn't what we need to figure this out. Maybe it's a local cop who'll think like a local cop."

He'd been waiting for the chance to put his skills to good use. For years, he'd been SWAT, so he could get on board with Roxie's need to kick doors down. But for some reason, that wasn't what he thought Niall might be talking about. "Start with the bar?"

"See if you can get a local lead that we can pull. Who knows? It could unravel all the way to a terror cell."

So much for feeling over his head on an interagency federal taskforce. The work he'd been doing had been an odd mix of familiar and foreign.

He needed to work the case like a local cop and gather evidence. Truth was what you could produce the evidence to prove—like the historical accuracy of the Bible. He'd built his faith that way, because as a cop, he couldn't stand on a firm foundation of wishful thinking.

"Okay, we'll pay a visit to the bar as soon as it

opens. Unless you can get me the home address of a bartender who might know our dead guys."

"I'll get you something." Niall said, "Anything else?"

Liam didn't think much about the wisdom of opening his mouth, he just said, "A way to not tie myself in knots trying to protect Roxie."

Niall chuckled. "Yeah, I'm the wrong guy for that. But you know what I've realized? We don't get much in this world we can control. But it's a privilege to protect those we care about. To stand in the gap for them. Even if that's what they're doing for us—maybe especially if they reciprocate."

"Thanks, Niall."

"I'll be praying for both of you. And I know everyone else is. Dakota has us all on standby in case we need to respond." Niall paused. "But I think Dakota would run point from the office. Neema has a crate there that Pronto can use."

"Thanks." Roxie would probably love to see their dog if the team showed up, but Pronto also needed to heal. "Let me know if you get anything."

They ended the call, and Liam opened his Bible app. He played the audio version and leaned back, closing his eyes. Relaxing with what he was listening to while he tried to let go of the anxiety. Fear could keep a person safe, keep their instincts on track, and indicate when danger was coming. Anxiety warped everything, crossed wires, and generally caused havoc.

Roxie's phone buzzed on the table.

He reached for it on a reflex and got as far as seeing it was from Simon and the message was an image. He frowned, figuring it was something funny or encouraging.

A man's picture stared back at him from the screen. Dark blonde hair, late thirties maybe early forties. The guy looked rough, and not the kind of man he wanted to meet when he was unprepared.

Liam glanced at the closed bedroom door. Who was this guy?

The message from Simon said simply,

> This is what I got.

Liam marked the message *unread* and locked the phone. Whoever this guy was, Liam didn't need to create tension between them. What existed between him and Roxie was at the same time strong and extremely tenuous. He wasn't going to unnecessarily rock the boat, but that was also because if he needed to know something, she would tell him.

That guy on her phone wasn't either of the men who had threatened her life, and it wasn't Darwish. It could be nothing. It could be something. If he needed to concern himself with it, she would tell him so he could help her process it. Or so he could support her.

The bedroom door opened, and Roxie walked over, her bare feet almost silent on the carpet. She'd put on some clothes, but he wouldn't describe her as *dressed*. Neither was he, in only his shorts. She walked right up to him, straddled his knees and sat on his lap, curling up against his chest. "You're warm."

She let out a sleepy sigh he felt on his pec. "Why did you get up?"

Liam rubbed a hand up and down her back. "Just

making sure things are secure. And reading my Bible."

"Good idea."

Liam leaned over far enough to hit play again, and they sat in silence, while his app read a Psalm aloud. A while later, she stirred and got up, tipping his coffee cup so she could see inside. She took it to the single cup maker and brewed two fresh ones.

As she carried both back over and sat beside him—shame—his phone chimed. "Text from Niall. He got the home address for a bartender who might be able to give us info on the two guys who burned the cabin."

"We got a lead?" Her eyes practically flashed with the chance to do something. She reached for her phone but paused. "Not that I don't love peaceful, restful vacations."

Liam grinned. "Sure."

She looked at her phone, head bent to it. Intent on what she was seeing.

"Everything good?" He kept himself still, his tone inquisitive.

"I don't know yet." She sat stiffly, not looking at him. "But I'll keep you in the loop if you need to know."

"Great."

See? He had nothing to worry about. Just a back-from-the-dead terrorist and an unknown plot to destabilize the economy.

Pretty much the same old, same old.

TWELVE

Roxie walked out of the house first, the cleaned off Marshals star badge on her belt. They'd dug some things out of the cabin wreckage since the fire department had cleared the scene enough they could walk through it. Not much had been salvageable though. "At least we got something from the bartender."

Liam followed her to his SUV, parked at the curb. "We're not going to talk about the rest of it?"

She nearly tripped. She knew she was going to have to explain about the photo Simon had sent. How could he be talking about that, though? "The rest of what?"

Simon had aged an old photo of her brother and come up with a man almost an exact match to the face of the man she'd seen outside the cabin. During a time when it was clear there were multiple people watching her and Liam. So, her brother and the two guys who'd burned the cabin down?

At least Liam hadn't been forced to shoot her brother.

She wanted to talk to him first. If it was possible.

Ask him why he had faked his death and gone dark side.

Her brother was working with Darwish. There wasn't any other reasonable explanation. She wanted to rest on the idea that if the rest of her family had been around, they'd be disappointed in him. Ashamed even.

But they weren't, and her family hadn't been good like that. They weren't criminals—she hoped—but they weren't pillars of the community either.

Not like Liam's.

He came from honorable people. He knew when he married her what he'd been getting into. But still. It did sort of feel like she might've rushed him or duped him even. That had to be why he wanted a wedding.

To convince everyone else that the choice he'd made was all right. That he could handle it.

He didn't start the car. "How about that entire conversation?"

She shifted in her seat to face him. "What are you talking about?"

"The fact he wanted you to turn on the charm and ask for the intel." Liam's expression darkened, and she saw something like possessiveness in his eyes. But the healthy kind, which she knew because she'd seen the unhealthy kind up close and personal. "Probably wanted you to sit in his lap."

She could point out that she'd only ever done that with him. And never planned to do it with anyone else. She didn't make a habit of going around sitting in men's laps. Instead, she tipped her head to the side. "Really?"

"Don't play. You noticed."

"The only thing I noticed was how hot you are when you're being a fed." She kept her expression impassive. "And it worked, cause he gave us the intel."

The bartender had told them that the two men had partied with friends after hours up in the hills around the town, always into the wee hours of the morning.

"Hmm." Liam started the car and pulled away from the curb.

Roxie leaned over and whispered some promises in his ear she was definitely going to keep later.

He cleared his throat.

"So...back to the people trying to kill us...or destabilize the economy...or both." She sat back in her seat, a smile tugging at her lips. "Let's go check out this place they hung out."

She wanted to look at the photo again as he drove them to the place. She had to admit that after having no family for years, it was a little intoxicating to realize she had a brother, and he was out there. Nearby even.

But would she slap him, arrest him, or hug him if she saw him?

Maybe all three. She wasn't sure what order they would come in, though. How was she supposed to deal with her brother being back, something that was looking more and more likely, when he was probably going to end up someone they hunted?

Roxie stared out the window, tapping her foot on the floor mat. If she could contact Adam, maybe she could convince him to pass on intel. Be a double agent. That would give the US Attorney who'd be charging him the leverage to offer her brother a break due to his helpful actions.

Her mind didn't want to think about best case scenarios, though. It only wanted to think about her chasing him as a Marshal, running down her own brother as a fugitive. Which was, of course, ridiculous since no one would give her permission to go after him. It would be passed to a deputy who didn't have a personal connection to the fugitive in question.

Liam pulled off the highway onto a single lane asphalt road. At the end, the road opened to a wide driveway, the width enough for a vehicle to turn around. The property mostly abandoned looking, a couple of rusted out cars were parked in what amounted to the yard.

Behind the barn-like structure, the hillside was swallowed up by dense trees that would prove a problem if the area were touched by a wildfire.

Above the main level, in the eaves of the barn was a single window with a dingy-looking curtain.

Roxie walked over to the front door, which looked like it would slide back. Her boots crunched gravel, and the mountain breeze ruffled the ends of her hair, so she had to shove a couple of wild strands behind her ear. Now wasn't the time to regret cutting it so short she couldn't pull it back.

She stopped outside the door and glanced at Liam. They both pulled weapons from their holsters. Her mind had compiled what she could hear from inside without even thinking of it consciously. Instinct had her reaching for a way to protect herself.

She grabbed the handle and hauled the door to the side, spilling light into the interior of the barn. At the same time, a teen guy on an overturned bucket fell backwards. Two shot up. Some busted up laughing.

"Don't mess yourself with fright, East." The kid snickered, shoving hair back from his face with a flick of his head. "It smells bad enough in here."

While he taunted his friend, two girls at the far end of the room turned and scurried out the back door. The taunter didn't look impressed by that, and Roxie caught the same intent that she'd seen on her abusive ex and his brother. That my-way-or-the-highway thing some guys had when they thought everyone should do whatever they ordered.

Good thing they rushed away.

East righted himself and got to his feet, shooting his "friend" a dirty look. "Can we help you, officers?"

Roxie didn't have time to explain why he was wrong calling them that. "What are you guys doing here? Shouldn't you be at school?"

East half-shrugged. "Teacher in-service. No school today."

They were all probably sophomores, maybe juniors. She could confirm the story with the local high school, but this wasn't about these kids. Necessarily. They weren't going to haul all four of them to the nearest police station for questioning. Unless they got belligerent.

"Good thing you're here," Liam said. "Because I have a quiz, and you all look like smart kids. The kind that carry ID on them. So, show me a driver's license or student ID." He motioned with his fingers.

Faced with Sergeant O'Connell and the force of his command presence, three licenses appeared. Mr. Taunting took a little longer. Once he had all of them, Liam took photos with his phone.

"We didn't do nothin'." East shifted his weight from foot to foot.

All the boys were in shorts and T-shirts, sneakers on their feet. The typical teenage trend that made it look like they were in uniform. She'd never belonged to that tribe. High school had been a case of keeping her head down. These days, she had a more solid handle on who she was and her individual style.

"I never said you did." Liam handed back their IDs. "Tell me about the two guys who crash here. They kind of run the place, right?"

Maybe they didn't know if the men were dead or not. Roxie wondered if using their names might get more information. Were they connected to the two men? Finding out they were dead might cause an adverse reaction that would derail them getting answers.

Liam glanced at the one who'd taunted East. "Hayden?"

The kid shrugged. "Sure, they run the place. But they said we can hang whenever."

"Until last week," East muttered.

Roxie said, "What happened last week?"

Hayden shifted his weight from foot to foot. East said, "They were acting all weird about us coming over. Saying we need to stay away. Now the storeroom is padlocked."

"They ain't here." Hayden shrugged. "I don't see what the big deal is." He eyed her and Liam. "Did they call the cops? They snitches now?"

Roxie said, "They aren't using us to kick you out." As if she needed to maintain the reputation of a couple of local criminals. "Any idea what changed? Did they get into something?"

Hayden shrugged. "How should we know?"

The two who'd been quiet did the same but said nothing. Now it was East who looked squirrely.

Roxie stepped closer to the kid but wasn't prepared to do more than what it took to get him to focus on her from where he stood. "What were they into?"

"Now I'm supposed to give them up?" He sniffed, releasing some of the tension with a roll of his shoulders. In the process, he glanced to the padlocked door at the far end of the room. "I don't know anything. So it's not like you can arrest me."

"That's right." One of the quiet ones spoke up. "You can't arrest us. That means we're free to leave whenever we want."

Roxie shrugged. They had the kids' IDs, so they could follow up officially with an adult present if they needed any further information. "Have a good day."

They all trailed out, leaving the debris of their attempt at a good time around where they'd been gathered. Empty beer cans, chip bags, and a few cigarette butts.

Liam wandered through the room. She watched the open door and saw the kids head on foot down the lane, then she joined him just as he took bolt cutters to the padlock. It clanged on the floor, and Liam leaned the tool against the wall before easing the door open.

He pushed it wide, standing with her at the door so they could both look in. "Huh."

Roxie stared at the interior. "You might have to explain this to me." It didn't look like a meth lab, or some other kind of drug production setup. Maybe electronics, like computers? There were circuit boards, wires, and white drums of... "Wait, is this to make a bomb?"

Liam shivered.

She touched his arm and stepped in. Benson had been hit with a number of explosive devices. He had nearly died, and several cops who'd been friends had lost their lives in a deadly drive by shooting. Liam wasn't far behind her.

"Don't touch anything. Someone is gonna want to go over this as evidence."

Roxie nodded. "Noted." She didn't have a whole lot of expertise on bombs that weren't simply C4 and a detonator. This looked complicated, with timers and mixing chemicals. Someone had cooked something in a huge pot over a camping burner. "What do you think?"

"I think I'm gonna call this in. Because we have the makings of several bombs that are no longer here, and they're not the kind that took out the train."

Roxie glanced over at him. Someone had made different bombs here than the type used to blow the train? Hadn't that one been little more than sabotage, the evidence of how it blew up in flames?

He put his phone to his ear. "We have a serious problem on our hands."

THIRTEEN

"Okay, will do." Liam hung up the phone, that odd note of discomfort in him still just as strong as it had been before. He couldn't shake the feeling Darwish was up to something, and it was going down here—or close enough that multiple explosive devices had been constructed here. Probably transported out.

Roxie circled the room, still not touching anything. He wasn't ever not aware of where she was or what she was doing, but he figured that was the nature of being married.

He dumped the photos he'd taken in the folder Talia had told him to use. The pictures of the licenses for the teen boys and the images he'd taken of the truck license plates outside, along with everything from in this room. He also shared his GPS location with her email address so she could check out who owned the land.

They would hopefully get a lead from somewhere.

"There's someone outside." Roxie pulled her gun and crept to the window to look out.

Liam went to the door to the main area. "What do you have?"

He peered out, assessing if there was more than one person here or if those teens had returned, while he listened.

Roxie said, "Caucasian, late thirties. Dark hair. Cargoes, boots, and a T-shirt. He's got a vest on over his T-shirt and a shirt over that. Not that he'd be able to disguise who he is."

Lethal. Liam spotted another man out front. This one looked Hispanic. "We're surrounded." And if they were going to get away, it would be by fighting their way out. The car was lost to them if multiple men were between them and the SUV. Men who had vests on, where he and Roxie didn't.

The image of a bullet tearing through her flashed in his mind, threatening to make him sick.

"Back door." They'd have it covered, but Roxie and Liam needed to hedge their bets against the smallest number of these men and just make a run for it rather than mounting an all-out offensive. He grabbed the door, closed it, and wedged a chair under the lock. It wouldn't hold for long.

"It'll have to be this window." Roxie shoved up the center crossbar of wood, then thumbed the latch and tried again. It eased up slowly and started to squeak.

"Can you see that guy?"

Roxie said, "Doesn't mean he isn't watching. Or that he won't hear the noise. We just need to move quickly because it's better than being sitting ducks." She looked out, glancing both ways. "Give me a boost."

She lifted her foot. Liam wanted to say he'd go

first, but that wouldn't cut down much on the danger to either of them.

He shoved up and out hard, and she tucked and rolled. Roxie didn't even grunt. She came up on one knee, her gun pointed straight out in front of her. Elbows loose. Scanning around them.

Liam levered himself out. As soon as his boots hit the ground, a round cracked off, slamming the wood by his shoulder, sending flying shards at him. "Go!" He ran to Roxie, dragged her up by her arm, and moved her so she was behind him. The idea that she could be killed when they had barely started their lives together wasn't something he wanted to entertain.

Fear was like a dragon stomping around the corners of his mind, shaking the foundations of what he knew to be true. The surety he was supposed to fall back on.

God... He didn't even know what to pray.

He only knew to run.

Liam raced between two trees. A heavy figure came at him fast, and Liam could only rotate toward the man before he was tackled.

His back hit the ground, and all the air expelled from his lungs. He managed to get enough breath in him to yell, "Roxie, run!"

Beyond the hulk of a man on him, he spotted her swing her arm down. Hot pain cut at his shoulder, on the outside of his arm. In the same moment, she slammed her gun into the man's head. He slumped down, and Liam pushed the guy off him to the ground.

"We need to move." They could circle around, watch for these people to leave, and then get to the car. It was that or figure out how to get out of here on foot.

A radio crackled, under the man between him and the ground. "Ash, is it done? Come back."

Roxie stared at the man lying face down.

Liam took her arms. "We have to go."

She shifted out of his hold, and he let her go. "I need to see who it is." Roxie shoved the man's shoulder, making him flop to his back. Out cold. "It's not him."

"There's no time to worry about that right now. We have to *move* before the rest of them catch up." He had no idea how many there were or how long they had. And yet, his mind still wanted to think about the photo of that man on her phone.

She was right. It wasn't him.

Maybe saying aloud that there was no time to worry about that right now was more him trying to convince himself. He scanned around them. "Come on. We can find a spot to hide."

She turned to him, and they set off, moving away from the back of the barn. Into the dense trees that would thankfully provide some decent cover. He watched in case someone else came up behind them. In case there was another person in the woods around them waiting for a sneak attack.

He lifted his arm enough to see the wound on the outside of his shoulder and the slice in his T-shirt. Blood dripped down his arm.

She switched her gun hand and held his left with her right hand. Sacrificing the accuracy she'd worked hard to compensate for with the need to hold on.

Because he would protect her.

No matter what she had going on that she hadn't

shared with him, there was nothing powerful enough it would tear them apart. Not after what they'd been through to get here.

Liam glanced back over his shoulder. Firing his weapon with the same arm that was bleeding wouldn't feel good, but it was the same trade off Roxie made. Unless they totally switched sides, but that meant overthinking this thing. "Hold up."

He took a couple of steps and stumbled against a tree, sucking in breaths.

Roxie gasped. "You're bleeding." She rushed over, holding his elbow while she looked at the cut. "I saw him swipe out, but I didn't know he cut you!" She kept her voice at a furious whisper.

"I'm good." And that wasn't some macho declaration. He touched the side of her neck, rubbing his thumb on her jawline. "I'm good, Rox."

She came close, pressing all the way up against him. His back to the tree. Her in front of him. All that fire, independence, and strength. The dragon of fear slowed to a stop and seemed to diminish with the feel of being surrounded.

Roxie touched her lips to his. He fought to keep his senses listening for someone approaching them, knowing she was freaked out and trusting him to take care of them. The way she'd taken care of him with that guy just now.

He wanted nothing more than to fall into the kiss and lose himself. Being married wasn't easing the need to spend time with her, shutting out the world and just being together. Might even be making it worse. But there were problems out in the world outside the two of them that needed to be solved.

Liam eased off and touched his forehead to hers.

He turned his head slightly, not losing any part of the connection with her. She was like peace in the storm, giving him a stillness—contentment—he'd never known. A gift of God that could be a reflection of the true peace he found in Jesus. All this solid foundation was a little unnerving after feeling off kilter for years. He was going to have to get used to feeling this way.

Thank You.

For years, all he'd had was the dream of what it would've been like with her. The ways they would have supported and loved each other.

Now he knew he'd been right, and it was sweet.

"See anyone?" She clung to him, letting him judge the situation.

"No, but I hear them. We should keep moving."

She hesitated, then nodded. Liam's mind wanted to read into why she might want to know more about the people after them. Because of her photo.

Instead of letting his thoughts spiral back to that, he eyed her. "What read did *you* get from that guy?"

"Right?!" She pulled away, still keeping her voice low, and set off between the trees to the side of what looked like a deer path. "It did seem odd. Almost...tactical."

"So, mercenaries?" He didn't like the idea that Darwish had more men. Or that it was the group the CIA had lost track of. "Maybe since we killed the last two, they sent a team with a greater chance of survival."

"That makes sense." She stepped off a rock onto the dirt, picking her way. "Escalating because they got a read that we're not just going to roll over and die."

Liam had zero intention of doing that. "He can't believe we would. Darwish has seen us in action." The guy was probably laughing himself sick at the fact they thought they'd killed him. What on earth had he been doing for all these years?

Recruiting deceased operatives and spies. If no one was looking for the men he brought on, they could do whatever they wanted under the radar. There could be an entire network of people no one was looking for out there causing who knows what kind of mayhem.

"Let's go." She tugged on his arm, and they kept moving. "Are we going in a circle? I should check my maps app and see where we are, because I have no idea what's over this ridge. I'm just heading for high ground."

Usually that was a solid plan. "It'll be a while before they give up and leave. I'm not sure I want to waste that much time waiting when we could find another way back to our hotel and regroup. Get the car later."

"I don't think a rideshare driver is gonna want to get shot at. Or stabbed."

"True." He chuckled.

She had her phone out. Liam scanned behind them, down the hill, and spotted at least three men fanned out coming up the incline. Still at least a quarter mile away.

"There's a river ahead of us."

"Good. Let's run to it because they're coming." He nudged her, and they set off. Thankfully, the lives they led meant they could keep pushing through, using the physical strength they'd honed with years of workouts and physical labor. They both stayed in shape.

A bullet sang through the air.

Liam hissed between clenched teeth. "Already bleeding, guys!"

They picked up their pace, tearing between trees. Roxie crossed the deer track and leaped over a downed tree. She stumbled. "It's a drop off!"

Liam slammed into her back. Their friends had gone off a cliff into a river and barely survived running from bad guys. River and Tessa had survived, though. *Some of that favor would be good right now, if You'd be so inclined to lend a hand.*

There was no time to pray for the long list of things he needed, like wisdom and discernment.

He glanced back once, saw them gaining on him. They hadn't shot at her. That guy had only gone after him. He made a split-second decision and shoved at her, saying, "Go south. Meet me at the car."

And then he jumped over the edge.

FOURTEEN

Roxie's mind took a second to assimilate what had just happened. Multiple of those mercenary guys were coming. Liam had dived down the edge of that steep incline. Not exactly a vertical cliff but close enough he'd have to be seriously careful. As she watched, he grabbed a tree branch and wrenched his shoulder turning himself around.

He stopped, facing the top of the hill, his boots making deep ruts in the dirt. Behind him, rocks and debris scurried down the hill. He was about fifteen feet down, and it looked like he was getting ready to face off with these guys.

The odds were bad.

South. That was what he'd told her.

She started running. Those guys might follow her. She would be able to draw them away from her husband. *Please, Lord.* Roxie needed to figure a way out of this that left both of them alive.

But if these guys wanted to massacre her and Liam, they'd have shot them dead already. It wouldn't be that hard to kill them with overwhelming force.

She and Liam were outnumbered. Why hadn't they simply attacked?

Instead, it seemed more like they were focused on Liam—and using nonlethal force.

The decline was a whole lot more manageable farther down. Roxie didn't think it through too much, she just ran over the edge and did the same thing Liam had by grabbing a tree in order to slow her descent and turn her around.

She ran horizontally back toward Liam, switching gun hands again because her grip was starting to cramp. Each breath came fast, one after the other. She pushed one out and held it for a second, matching her breathing to her pace the way she did when she went for a run.

"Lee!"

He glanced at her, frowning when he saw her coming.

"Pick your way over here." She stumbled, grabbed a tree, and went down on one knee.

He wanted to argue. She could see it in the expression on his face. Beyond him, a man appeared at the top of the ridge.

Roxie swept her arm up and aimed. She squeezed off two shots that hit the man's vest. He tumbled over the edge toward Liam.

Her husband scrambled along the steep cliff, his feet sinking into the earth which started to slide as he waded over. A slab of dirt and rocks from the surface slipped from where he had been a second before.

She grasped the tree and gritted her teeth. *Jesus, don't let him fall.*

He picked up his pace as the cliff leveled out some and the drop off wasn't quite as sheer, finding what was probably an animal path on the decline toward her.

She wrapped her elbow around the tree and switched her gun to that hand, holding out her other.

He grabbed her hand, interlocking their thumbs to clasp each other's wrists. "Why did you double back?"

"Why did you sacrifice yourself?"

They just might be at odds about that for the rest of their lives. But at least this way, they'd both be around to keep hashing it out for years to come.

"Let's go." She let go of the tree and found her footing, then proceeded to race along the shallow drop. The decline continued to gentle the farther they got from where he had leaped over the edge.

Her breath caught in her chest.

She'd actually watched him dive and thought for a second that he was falling to his death. Leaving her there. At least she'd figured out his plan rather than thinking he was saving himself. But they were better off sticking together.

She didn't want them to be apart. Not for a while.

She'd already had to leave her dog behind to come on this trip. Being by herself wasn't going to give her any peace in the middle of all that was happening.

She crested the edge and glanced back. The men were up at the spot where their teammate had fallen. Good. She'd hit his vest, so he wasn't dead, but they were distracted pulling him back up the cliff.

That could give them the edge they needed to get away.

Roxie ran flat out in the direction of the barn, first down the grassy hill in a circle around where they'd run up it, and then on a path that stretched out like a beacon.

She prayed they weren't going to meet someone up ahead like that guy who'd tackled Liam.

From the sound of his boots, he ran pretty close behind her. *Good.* Together was good. She wanted to reach back and take his hand again, but with how fast they were going, it would be awkward to be tethered like that.

Roxie breached the tree line and immediately circled left around the barn. Gun ready, just in case, but running this hard, she'd have to aim first.

Liam gave her an order her brain barely registered.

She managed to follow it, slowing enough that she could stop at the front corner of the building. Clearing in front of them, multiple vehicles. Two rusted out trucks to the left. A man strode out of the main barn door they'd dragged open.

She looked back and indicated what she'd seen with hand signals.

Liam nodded, and then went first. *Of course.* There wasn't any point in arguing, and she liked that his instinct was to care for her by being a protector. As her husband and her superior—and formerly her team leader—it was his role in more ways than one.

Arguing could get them killed.

Just like stopping to find out if any of these men knew her brother also could. But the fact that it might confirm her brother as both alive and working for a dangerous man wasn't something she was ready to absorb. Would she ever be?

Liam jumped the man from behind and punched him in the side of the head. The man dropped to the ground under him, but Liam straightened. "Come on. It won't be long before the others catch up."

In fact...

She barely glanced back long enough to see more than one man step from between the trees and took off after Liam. "Go. Go. Go."

He ran around to the driver's side of his SUV. Roxie heard the locks beep and dragged the door open. A couple of shots hit the back corner of the car.

Liam hit the gas and peeled out in a spray of gravel. She grabbed the bar at the top of the open door while he circled around in a tight turn between the other vehicles and the barn. He bumped onto the grass and cut a path around, then back on the road down the hill.

Roxie slammed the door, breathing hard. The pounding heart and airy breaths in her ears dissipated, and she realized the radio was up loud. She reached over and turned it down.

"We're gonna talk about that."

She glanced over at Liam, buckling her seatbelt. "Put your belt on." As he complied to her yelled order, she said, "You bet we are." Roxie could spit she was so mad. She wanted to wring his neck about shoving her away like that so he could face those guys single-handedly. "What were you thinking? You couldn't have taken them all on alone."

He just shrugged one shoulder. "They wouldn't have been expecting me right below them. They thought I fell."

"*I thought you fell!*"

He reached over and squeezed her knee. "It's all good, Rox."

Because she'd come back for him. That was why

he was currently alive. She was mad enough to consider the merit of having left him behind to take care of that solo.

She gritted her teeth together. Sweat coated her, dampening her shirt and making her uncomfortable. Water in the console gave her something to focus on rather than the desire to wring his neck right now. When she'd downed the entire bottle and tossed it on the floor in the back, she said, "Don't do that again."

He glanced over. "You were scared."

She leaned toward him. "Don't. Do. That. Again."

"Okay." He reached for her hand and held onto it.

Roxie closed her eyes and tried to control her breathing the way she'd done when she was running. Maybe it was that she didn't want to face the truth about her brother, and she hadn't read Liam into that yet. The impending blow up about why she'd hidden that from him left a sour taste in her mouth. Was she projecting?

Tit-for-tat wasn't how compromise was found.

If he was going to accuse her of withholding her suspicions, she didn't need what just happened as ammo to fight back with.

Conflict would only start a war. Compromise and backing down would help build a peace treaty.

Liam shifted in his seat enough to pull out his phone. "Answer that, will you?"

She took the phone. The screen said, *The Office* so she put it on speaker. "O'Connell." Getting used to answering the phone with that still hadn't happened. "We're both here."

"It's T."

Liam glanced from her back to the road. "Hey, Talia. What's new?"

"Why do both of you sound out of breath?"

Roxie said, "We had a run in with some guys. Tricked out, rough looking but like military. Or former." Presumed dead or declared missing in action.

She explained all of it, from the teens to the bombs to the men chasing them. When she was done, she had to catch her breath.

"All righty, Marshal. Sounds like you had a full day."

Roxie caught a note in Talia's tone. They hadn't worked together much, but she was gathering the fact that her first inclination had been correct. Talia had a huge well of compassion in her. Along with being crazy good with computers—like Simon Olson level good—she also had more style in one painted pinky nail than Roxie had in her whole body. Then she'd taken note of Roxie's lack of style, and they'd gone shopping three days after meeting each other.

Now Roxie had a bunch of jackets and boots that she loved.

She said, "But you have something for us?"

Talia didn't waste a second. "I ran the information you sent, Lee. Driver's licenses didn't come back with anything but one DUI that got dropped. Somebody's daddy is a lawyer. But the trucks parked at the barn were more interesting."

Roxie said, "The rusty ones?"

"Yep, those."

Liam squeezed her hand and let go to tuck a stray strand of hair that had come loose from his short ponytail back behind his ear. "Who do they belong to? Anyone we know?"

Talia said, "An eighty-two year old man who lives down in Riverside, in So-Cal. He owned the property years ago but moved south into a retirement home so his kids could have him close but never visit him."

Roxie frowned.

"If my children don't visit me when they put me out to pasture, I'll ruin their credit."

Liam chuckled. "Sure you will."

Apparently, she wouldn't do that. Roxie said, "Anything else?" Could be the team wanted them to drive down and talk to the guy.

"According to *his* credit," Talia said, "he rented three panel vans two days ago."

"Three." Liam's tone lowered. "As in, our bombs? Darwish could've used the three to transport what they constructed at the barn."

"Bombs in vans?" Roxie hadn't seen one by the train, and no one had mentioned it. But someone could've driven a device to the train in one and then carried it on board.

"And one has already gone off. Which means there are two more out there." Liam paused.

Talia picked up where he left off. "I called the rental company and I'm waiting for a call back. I'll see if they have GPS, and if they do, I'll let you know where to find them. We'll call everyone if we have to. Make sure no one else gets hurt."

"Thanks, Talia." Roxie bit her lip. "Call when you have something."

She hung up the phone and looked at her own.

No new notifications.

Were they about to experience the calm before the storm?

FIFTEEN

Liam drove most of the way back to the hotel, making loops in town to ensure they weren't being followed. His phone buzzed. "It's Dakota." Liam handed over his phone.

"She sent an address. We're supposed to go check it out." She tapped the dash screen. "I'll get directions started."

"Thanks." He gripped the wheel.

Since they'd hung up with Talia, neither of them had said much. Too lost in their thoughts. Her reaction to his choice to separate and face those guys by himself was like a cloud in his mind. He couldn't see through it to figure out what was going on.

Sure, he understood the fear of not knowing what would happen to him. The fact he'd have been going up against that many armed men wasn't something he'd thought too much about, or he probably wouldn't have done it. If she wanted him to refuse to give his life to protect her, they weren't going to agree. Because he would give it. Anytime, any day. If it kept her alive, he would absolutely take that risk.

Wouldn't she do the same?

They were both wired to do it. But then, they were also wired to go in together, take care of the problem watching each other's backs, and not leave the other behind.

Was that what he'd gone against?

Maybe being married and partners had more potential for problems than he'd realized. He was a guy. Did he have to have all the ins and outs of issues that might crop up figured out? He was far more inclined to deal with problems as they came up than worry about what might not happen.

He pulled up to a stoplight and glanced over. "Doing all right?"

She nodded, not looking nearly as exhausted as he felt. They'd both tumbled through the dirt, but she managed to look good even with the smudges and the rumpled clothing. He needed a shower.

"So where are we headed?"

"Dakota didn't say what it was." She swiped her phone, making him think of that picture Simon had sent her. "But the address is a local municipal airport. I'll ask if there's more intel to know."

"Great. Thanks." He said, "Ask about Pronto as well. Is she okay?"

"They went for a long walk this morning. She's sleeping now."

Liam reached over and squeezed her knee, then set off when the light turned green. Trees flanked both sides of the road, planted in cut outs in the sidewalk, creating a natural feel to this downtown area. Cafes had outdoor seating, and the place had a bustling feel to it. Still, the air was relaxed like a vacation.

Something he wasn't sure they'd managed to have yet.

They'd run for their lives and nearly been killed more than once. If he wanted to get Roxie to learn how to let go of her fears, this probably wasn't how to go about it. This week had been a trial-by-fire so far. "It's okay to be scared, you know."

He wondered if she would respond, but finally, she did. "I'm scared something might happen to you."

"That's normal, I think." Liam said, "We walked a long road to get here. Neither of us wants to lose that."

Wide open landscape became scattered buildings, then a resort complex with a wide drive and manicured shrubs. Beside it was a pool, then beyond that, tennis courts followed by a hotel.

Roxie said, "If something happens to me, you have your family and the team." She fell silent, and he waited her out, wanting to know what she had to say. "If something happens to you..." She cleared her throat. "What do I have?"

Her lack of family wasn't lost on him. "You have everyone I have. Because you're part of them now."

If she didn't know that, then she'd be able to find that reassurance, right? Maybe that was precisely why they needed a wedding reception party. So their friends and family could officially claim her, and she would see just how much they loved that she was now part of the family.

Her phone buzzed. "Dakota said the address showed up on a scanner. Someone called the police, and it was flagged because it has airplanes and a white panel van."

So it could be another attack? He drove faster, in

case doing so saved a life. He had a beacon for emergency lights that would sit on his dash if he needed to use it, but for now, he left it in the glove box. When he glanced over next, she was looking at the image he'd seen on her phone.

Liam figured now or never. "Who is he?"

"Oh." She paused.

Liam kept his focus on the road, so she didn't feel like he was pinning her down even though that was exactly what he was doing.

"He's my brother."

Liam frowned.

"He was Army." She paused again. "Killed in action when I was fourteen. The dog I had in high school? That was his dog."

And her best friend. He'd been killed when a boyfriend Roxie had backed out of her drive in his truck in a hurry to leave and hit the animal.

Liam reached over to hold her hand, but she shifted in her seat so he set it on his lap. "Why do you have a picture of him?"

"I had Simon take the last picture the Army has of him and age it so I can see what he'd look like now. So that I could tell if it was the same man I saw outside the cabin the night before it burned."

Liam bit down on his molars. "Did you see him at the barn?"

She shook her head. "Just that once."

"Do you believe he's alive?"

He heard her breathy exhale, then she said, "I want to believe it as much as I don't. Because if it's true he's alive, then he works for Darwish."

"Was it accidental that you saw him, or did he let you?"

She made a "huh" sound. "He was just standing there. Right when I looked out." She shifted in her seat.

Liam glanced over. "He wanted you to see him."

"Why would he do that?"

If the guy was working for Darwish, he could feel torn, given family loyalty. Had Roxie's relationship with her brother been like that? "Back on the hill behind the barn... I'm not sure those men were trying to kill us."

"The one who attacked us just tackled you."

"At first, I wondered if it was simply because he considered me the bigger threat." Which wasn't true, given Roxie's skills. He might hit harder, but she could take a man bigger than her down to the ground if she had to.

"Are you still bleeding?"

He hadn't even thought about it. Now that he did, he realized it stung. "I don't think it's bad."

Liam felt the gentle touch of her fingers. Unfortunately, that included tugging a sticky part of his shirt away from the wound. "Sorry."

He gritted his teeth. "How does it look?"

"If you don't clean it up and at least get some butterfly strips on it, you'll have a nasty scar." She squeezed his triceps. "Good thing I dig scars."

The dash screen indicated they would be at the airport in less than five minutes. He spotted a sign shortly after, his head spinning with the problem of Roxie's brother. Most notably, whether it was, in fact, a problem. He wasn't sure since the guy hadn't tried anything. He also hadn't made an approach.

He glanced over. "What's your brother's name?"

"It was Adam." She shook her head. "I'm so used to thinking about him in the past tense."

"Maybe it was enough for him to just see you and for you to see him." Liam turned into the airport, mostly wire fences and plain gray hangars. "And that's all it's going to be. I mean, we don't even know if he was part of the group that chased us up that hill."

"I can't see how you don't think they were trying to kill us when that one cut you."

Liam heard the note in her voice. "He could've pulled his sidearm and shot me. If he had, I'd have pulled mine as well and reciprocated. So would you. Did you feel at any point like you needed to shoot him?"

"I hit him over the head because it's less paperwork."

"The fact you had time to consider that and react means you weren't scared for my life or yours. Not really."

Roxie said, "Huh."

But there wasn't time to talk about it more. They had arrived. "I don't see chaos or a commotion."

"The address is for a hangar up ahead, so keep going."

He followed her instructions, pulling through another gate and around to an open hangar with a shiny Learjet inside. An older man in blue coveralls tucked a yellow rag into his pocket and approached.

Liam parked and they both flashed their badges. "This is Deputy Marshal O'Connell. I'm Sergeant O'Connell. We're part of a taskforce." Which brought the customary explanation of why he was

PD, and they weren't regular cops or even normal feds. "You called in an incident?"

The older man frowned, the gristly stubble on his chin shifting with his jowls. The name patch on his overalls said *Stan*. "Police didn't do much but tell me to come down to the station and make a statement. What made it hit the radar of a taskforce?"

Roxie had her phone out. "The description you gave of the men you saw matches people we're looking for."

"Didn't just see them," Stan said. "Had a whole conversation. Nice boys. Bit intense, but they didn't hurt me or threaten anything."

Liam glanced around. Had they stolen something? "What made you call it in?"

"Questions they were asking me 'bout a certain area to the west of here. It's a no-fly zone, which I told them."

Liam frowned. "What no-fly zone?"

Stan hissed. "I only know cause I was Air Force. Worked some in a couple different places, higher than normal security clearance. But it's been long enough any information I have is outdated, so it's not like I'm a threat or someone who would know anything."

But men had shown up and asked questions about things he *did* know. Roxie said, "Can you describe them?"

Stan shifted his stance. "Military looking guys but civilian clothing. Cargoes. Big jackets like they were carrying weapons but had them out of sight. All of them big." He raised his hands, palms facing each other the width of Liam's shoulders. "Showed up not long before dawn. I'd have been scared if they meant me harm."

Liam glanced at Roxie who looked at him and nodded. The same guys from the barn, which meant they'd been busy. But what were they up to? He said, "What did they want to know about the no-fly zone?"

"Apart from how to get a plane in there without anyone detecting it?" Stan chuckled. "As if that was possible."

So, they wanted to fly into a place that was intended for no aircraft. By asking, they'd tipped their hand. Was it intentional?

Roxie said, "And you have no idea what's there?"

"I can guess as good as anyone, but I'd rather not find out and keep my life instead." Stan lifted a hand and wandered off.

Roxie turned to him. "What kind of area has a no-fly zone?"

"Somewhere they don't want anyone looking down and seeing what's happening." But that didn't really help him answer her question.

Or figure out how all this tied together.

SIXTEEN

Roxie flipped her hair forward and started to dry it with the towel, glancing between the short strands to see Liam watching her with an appreciative look on his face.

"Can you hear me?" The voice came through the computer speakers.

"Yeah, Niall," Liam said. "What've you got for us?"

"Roxie is there?"

She called out, "Yes!"

Liam smiled. "Everyone is connecting if you want to say hi."

She straightened. "Just need to brush my hair out." She hung up the towel and grabbed her hairbrush, going back to the living area of the suite in her bare feet. Jeans and a T-shirt. Liam had put his shoes back on, but she refused to live a life where she was dressed to run at any moment.

Even with what was happening, she needed to be able to switch off. Or at least trust that he had it covered. That she would have time to grab her gun and slide her feet into running shoes before they jumped off the balcony or whatever.

The likelihood of an attack was low. No one had come after them directly since the cabin.

Still, part of her wanted to figure a way to draw out her brother. If she could at least talk to him, then she would know how far gone he was.

"She figured it out?" Liam's brows rose.

Roxie slumped down onto the couch beside him and saw the screen. Dakota in one corner dialing in from home, then Talia in the office. Niall with the same background as Talia. Josh and his gorgeous German Shepherd in his vehicle, or so it looked.

Niall glanced to the side, then said, "Haley was looking into Darwish from before his 'death' and found a manifesto online that was written by his brother. The one we thought was so much better than him."

Talia's eyes refocused, and Roxie figured she was looking at something else but still listening. Maybe looking at something that related to what Niall just said. Or working on something of her own.

Roxie loved Haley, Niall's wife, who was a civilian employee for Homeland Security. Though lately she'd cut back on her hours to take care of their kids. She worked part time now. It was part of the reason Roxie had gone for federal agent rather than civilian employee. She would love to be a mother and planned to give that her full attention someday. But she just didn't want to take on too much at once.

She fully planned to enjoy this season working with Liam again. Doing the side-by-side thing.

For a while, anyway.

Not that she couldn't be a mother as well as a federal agent. Plenty of people were cops and parents. But she didn't have even Liam's family nearby to help if she did stick with it. There could be times they were out of town for weeks working a case.

Roxie's mom had left her. How would her child having an absent parent not feel the same, even when she always planned to come back?

Niall was still talking, but then he seemed to be done, and she realized she'd fully zoned out.

Liam said, "So the train, the plane, and the boat emojis mean attacks? Or is it simply a puzzle that will keep us chasing our tails?"

Roxie tried not to look completely confused. Simon hadn't returned her messages about whether there had been any sightings of her brother flagged by law enforcement, or if it was possible he was some kind of agent, and she was supposed to *think* he was dead.

Liam continued, "Like the train we were on that blew?"

"I'm not so sure about that." Niall shook his head. "The whole manifesto is about three coordinated strikes, though some versions of his mission statement have more and some have less. It's about causing catastrophic tectonic destabilization. Earthquakes, even tsunamis."

Roxie frowned. "On the west coast? That could send a tidal wave to Hawaii. Could it be big enough to submerge the islands?"

Dakota said, "If it does, that means California, Oregon, and Washington have some devastating problems on their hands."

So, losing Hawaii would be the least of their worries? Maybe not the least of some folks' concerns, just the people in the middle of what was happening here. It would all be about perspective—and empathy.

Dakota whistled the way Roxie had shown her, and Roxie got a motion alert on her phone. Pronto came over, jumping up on the couch—something Roxie would have to un-train because she didn't want dog hair on her clothes forever. Dakota gave the dog a treat from her pocket and told Pronto to "down," which she did with her chin in Dakota's lap. Probably waiting for another treat to appear.

Niall said, "The whole point of the plan is to devastate centers of affluence. He's got other plans for New York, Toronto, and a bunch of European cities. He was thorough."

Talia took over when he was done. "Darwish's half-brother, the one who took over after him and turned out to be worse, was captured by the US several years ago. Since then, he's effectively disappeared. He was listed on detainment paperwork under one of his assumed names. There's a brief I can't read—yet. I'll get into it, don't worry. But he basically disappeared."

"What does that mean?" Roxie asked them.

"I can try and find where he is, but if someone wants him buried, then he's going to be hard to track down." Talia effectively explained that disappeared meant *disappeared* but thankfully didn't put it like that.

"In the meantime, we can track down these bombs," Liam said. "Anything on the rental vans?"

The three rented by whoever's vehicles those had been at the barn. She turned to Liam. "Do you really think the bombs were made at that barn, and now Darwish is taking them to enact his brother's plan?"

The train had already exploded. It hadn't caused an earthquake.

But then, Darwish had told her on the phone that had been for fun.

He said, "They had to be pieces of larger devices. Maybe partially assembled components he's going to combine with explosive material."

She didn't like the sound of that. In fact, her stomach flipped over and she thought she was going to be sick. "Can Darwish get his hands on nuclear material or something that powerful?"

Niall winced. Josh petted his dog, who leaned against his chest. Even Dakota reached for Pronto for comfort. The idea of nukes wasn't a good thought. The means to kill millions in a way that would permanently wreck the country and devastate a considerable portion of the world?

Roxie shivered. Liam reached over and held her hand, whispering, "We'll figure it out."

The fact her brother might be on board with Darwish's plan would end up a footnote if this thing actually went down.

It was unbelievable.

Niall said, "It seems Darwish may very well be enacting his brother's plan."

Something niggled at her about the brother, though. "What do we know about the no-fly zone?" The fact there was one of those in the middle of northern California was interesting enough she wanted to dig a little. But when did that end well?

Talia said, "What if it's a black site?"

Everyone shifted. Dakota actually flinched.

Roxie said, "Like a secret prison? Could that be where the brother disappeared to?" Wouldn't that be a heck of a coincidence? Or it was exactly what Darwish wanted for his plan to go down.

"That makes sense," Talia said. "As much as I'd rather it didn't."

"Thank goodness those guys went to the airport asking questions, otherwise we never would've known it was there. Or that it was relevant to this." Liam's voice had an odd note.

"You're being sarcastic?" Maybe she just had water in her ears still.

"No way would we have found it otherwise. Asking about a place like that?" He shook his head.

"We're assuming it's the guys from the barn, right?" When he nodded, she said, "Niall, is it possible to get photos of my brother's team in the Army? From before he died. I'd like to see what they all looked like."

Niall nodded. "On it."

"If it is a black site, there will be some indications outside, right?" Roxie glanced from the laptop screen to Liam, and back. "We could take a drive."

Dakota smiled. "If you walk up and knock on the door, they'll shoot you."

"Who says I'll knock?"

Dakota chuckled. "Don't get shot."

"Here's the team, at least according to the Army," Niall said.

The screen flickered, and a series of photos popped up. Guys in their mid-twenties, two African-American, one Asian or Pacific Islander, one awkward looking guy with red hair and acne scars, and two Caucasian guys—one of which was her brother.

"That's not them." Liam squeezed her knee.

"Two are still alive, according to the social services office and the Veteran's Administration." Niall said, "I'll make contact. Ask if they know anything."

Roxie nodded. "Thanks."

She and Liam were closest to this secret location. Which might just turn out to be a military base that had nothing to do with Darwish's brother's plans. But then again, for all they knew, it was a place where they refined uranium into weapons grade material.

The only way they would find out if it was connected would be to go there and check it out.

And try not to get shot.

Plus possibly find her brother.

"What if the airport thing was about handing us a lead we wouldn't have pieced together...but for a different reason." She tapped her foot on the carpet. "What if he is in over his head and he wants out?"

"He's definitely in over his head." Liam's expression remained pretty blank, and there was no time to discuss what he was thinking.

She wanted to help her brother if she could. Despite the fact he might be a very different man than the young adult she had known years ago, that didn't mean he should be forgotten. No one was too far gone that they couldn't be helped.

Because that was what had happened to her.

She'd been at rock bottom, and her friends, and Liam most of all, had reached out and helped her. So what if Destiny had kind of forgotten about her through everything that happened? Roxie didn't think she could blame her friend for being too preoccupied to text back or reach out when she needed it.

She wasn't going to believe that she was the vulnerable one who needed others' help while not everyone did. Everyone needed it sometimes. It was the nature of being human to not be solitary, but to need to connect with others—or God.

"If we find him," Roxie said, "we'll be able to talk to him. Then we'll know a lot more about what's going on than we do now." Did she need to say it?

Liam shot her a look. "I need to put aside my overprotective tendency and work the case because the fate of half the country is at stake?"

She folded her arms. "Yes."

Niall said, "Who does this remind you of?"

Dakota chuckled. "No comment."

Josh looked like he was asleep, though Neema kept watch over him. Talia was still working on whatever had her attention while she listened, the corner of her mouth curled up.

Roxie loved the idiosyncrasies of this family unit and how they worked. It was so much different than anything else she'd been part of. She was a Marshal, but they all brought their unique skills. She prayed she felt like she fit with them soon, the way they seemed to fit with each other.

Speaking of which. "I guess it's time to put my Marshal training to good use."

"Is this where I get to make a joke about her being a manhunter?" Niall grinned.

Liam ignored it. "You think your brother is asking for help?"

"I think we won't know until we find him." It was the quickest way to get answers.

"Fine." He looked at the laptop. "Talia, any read on what that location is?"

As far as Roxie was concerned, they would find the answer to that question when they got there.

SEVENTEEN

Liam lay with his chest to the grass near the top of the hill. Above them, clouds obscured the night sky. Roxie lay next to him, her elbows on the dirt looking through the scope of a rifle. Liam lifted the binoculars and scanned. "I see at least four guys walking the fence."

He heard an exhale, and she said, "One building, two stories, but there's definitely more underground. You can see the ventilation exhaust in the corner by that shed."

"Guard shack."

"Huh?"

He'd been mulling it over. "It's a black site, right? I'm leaning more and more to this place being a prison."

"Maybe it's a secret research facility?"

Liam shuddered. Niall had told him the crazy story of him and Haley, and how they'd been trapped together in a place like that. It almost reminded him of the facility in Benson that he'd rescued Roxie, her friend, and his mom from. "I guess it could be, though I don't want to go find out."

"Same if it's a prison."

"In fact, I can honestly say there's a lot of places I'd rather be right now than on a hill overlooking some secret the government is trying to keep."

That was the difference between federal and local policing. With local law enforcement, it was all about bad guys and bringing them to justice. Working with the Northwest Counter Terrorism Taskforce meant sometimes the lines between good and bad blurred. Things weren't so cut and dry when the government they were supposed to respect and live under might be the ones not doing the right thing here.

"Like we should go to Hawaii?"

Liam chuckled. "Guess we'll have to wait for Blake and Violet's wedding for that one. Assuming we stop Darwish from enacting his brother's plot."

"Yeah, we should save Hawaii first."

The stakes were higher than when he did local police work also. Instead of knowing and living alongside the people he was safeguarding, it was now unnamed millions. The reach was far greater if they succeeded, which meant their work had a bigger impact.

A note of something hit his awareness.

"So, what now? Wait for morning and shift change, or see if people show up for work?"

Liam kept still, speaking low. "We could try and get close enough to take pictures." He listened for a second, then said, "Or we can ask them ourselves."

"Weapons down, hands up." The voice was solid steel.

Liam didn't even think about not complying. Did his voice sound like that when he needed it to?

Roxie lifted both hands to either side of her head and rolled onto her back away from the rifle. She sat up. Liam did the same in the other direction. He didn't like being separated from her, even when it was only a couple of feet. He also didn't want to get shot.

He stared up at the one in charge. "Can we help you guys?"

The others stood ready, hands on their rifles. All of them were soldiers, and they had far better gear than anything Liam and Roxie had used in the Marines.

Four guys, shining the flashlights on their rifles into Roxie and Liam's eyes. Completely ruining the night vision he'd gained being out here the last half an hour. The fifth guy was the one in command given the way he stood. "It's us who ask the questions. Got it?"

"Sure." He kept his hands raised and didn't move.

"Let's start with who you are."

Roxie said, "We have ID."

"You reach for it, we will shoot you. Keep your hands where they are."

Roxie nodded. Liam said, "We're cool. It's all good."

"Good." The guy lifted his chin. "Who are you guys?"

Roxie glanced over at him, so Liam said, "I'm—"

"Liam O'Connell." One of the soldiers shifted his stance. "Took me a minute to remember. Is that Anne Helton?"

Liam frowned at the guy. "Do we know you?" He stepped forward, and Liam got a look at his face. It took him a second, then he said, "Salty?"

One of the guys chuckled.

"So you do know each other?" the commander said.

Liam frowned. "Do any of you have rank or patches on your uniforms?" He couldn't see any indicators of what unit this might be.

"What did I say about questions?"

Liam sighed. He stayed quiet while the Marine he'd served with for a while explained who they were and how they knew each other. He referred to Liam as "solid" which made him feel good and would hopefully smooth things with these guys so he and Roxie could get off the ground.

When Salty was done, Liam picked up where he'd left off. "I became a cop. Roxie bounced around. We got married, and now, she's a US Marshal, and we're attached to an inter-agency taskforce."

The commander snapped out, "Which one?"

Roxie said, "Northwest Counter Terrorism."

Salty shifted. "Uh, you ain't in the northwest, bro. This is California."

"Yeah, we know," Liam said. "We stumbled on a threat in process. Were you with us when we went after General Darwish? We have reason to believe someone might be intending to come here. Maybe to cause trouble? We don't have much intel, which is why we're here doing recon."

"You don't need to worry. We've got the place secure."

Liam really *really* wanted to ask if this place was a detainment center. "How many people would be at risk if you were breached?"

"By someone other than you?"

The commander wasn't going to give them any

information, was he? Liam said, "In the event of a... problem... we could possibly lend a hand."

"I'd call my commanding officer for reinforcements."

"And how long would that take?" Where was the nearest base, anyway? Probably the one hours south of here. "Roxie and I are here *now*."

"Not to worry. The threat as you call it was already taken care of."

Liam shifted because his backside had started to go numb on the ground. He did his best to ignore the huge disadvantage they were in being on the ground with these guys standing over them. They weren't unarmed, but that didn't give them power here. "What happened?"

The commander chuckled. "We did our jobs. That's what happened. Got it?"

Right.

A boom rang out across the valley below. Everyone flinched. Salty got low in a crouch. The commander was moving before Salty stood back up, going to the edge to look out.

Liam twisted around to see a ball of fire flare up into the sky. Two pickup trucks slammed into the front gate. A grenade launcher from the bed of one of the trucks shot another projectile across the yard and hit the side of the building.

The commander called orders to his men, who took off running. "Who are these people?" He glanced between Liam and Roxie. "What are they here for?"

He took a shot in the dark. "Let me take a wild guess and say you're detaining Carim Ismael Darwish."

"They don't have names." The commander's attention flicked to the battle going on in the valley.

"Then I need to get my phone out so I can show you a picture."

"I've never seen their faces. That's not how this facility works." His gaze shifted again.

Roxie said, "We can help out if we all go down the hill. Make sure this ends the way your previous incident did."

Liam realized then that she hadn't shown an ounce of fear this entire time.

"You wanna go catch a bullet, be my guest." The commander waved an arm out.

They could have overpowered him, given it was two against one. Still, at least one of them would've been hurt in the process no matter how they went about it.

Roxie got up, drawing her sidearm as she moved, and raced down the hill.

The commander glanced at him. "Your wife?"

Liam got up. "Yep."

"Guess we should catch up with her."

Good idea. Liam set off running. As he raced down the hillside, he heard the commander behind him, barking orders into a radio. Getting intel and giving back instructions on their offensive effort. Liam had a pistol, and he planned to use it.

So long as none of these friendlies shot at him or Roxie.

He pulled the metal badge from his back pocket and managed to slide it on his belt without falling on his face. "Roxie, badge!" Hopefully she heard him and got her Marshal star on display so the military guys would know she was friendly.

The commander yelled, "Both of you stay out of the buildings," and sprinted past Liam through the gate. He fired a burst of shots at the pickup truck.

More men than should've fit in those trucks had infiltrated this base. A few ran across the yard to an open door. Others hunkered down, shooting at military guys.

There wasn't much cover.

Roxie took a knee and fired two shots. Then another two. In the space between, she got enough information to make a judgment call and glanced at him. "Inside."

"Go." Which meant he would follow her.

Always.

A shot snapped past his ear. Liam gritted his teeth while his long strides ate up the yard to the open door. Inside, a flash bang went off.

Roxie slammed into the wall beside the door, covering him against whoever came out. He slowed only slightly and ran inside going way too fast. There was no stopping his momentum.

Liam slammed into a man in jeans and a T-shirt. Dark features and a heavy jacket. The man flung back onto the floor and lifted a rifle.

Liam put two shots in his chest, and the rifle clattered to the floor.

Someone down the hall called out a command for him to identify himself. Liam called back, "Federal agents, coming in!"

Behind them, the battle continued to rage outside.

Sure, the commander had told them to stay out of any buildings, but those men had run in here. If they were going to get answers, it would be inside. They might end up in jail, or in a place like this, after they learned what was being hidden from regular citizens, but they would also have saved the west coast and potentially millions of lives.

Was Darwish here, breaking out his brother from prison so they could do this together?

The attack a few nights before that the commander had mentioned might've been to test their security—or their response time. It put everyone on alert at the facility but also let their attackers know what they'd be dealing with.

They ran down the hall and turned the corner. A Marine sat slumped on the floor with his back to the wall, holding the blood soaked shirt over his abdomen with both hands. Roxie knelt beside him. "Let's take a look."

His eyes rolled back in his head.

She looked up at Liam, a slight shake of her head. "He needs an ambulance in the next thirty seconds."

"Maybe there's a medical facility on site?" That was the best they could do. But it would also slow them down to get this guy where he could be saved.

"I'll stay with him. You go look." She twisted around in her crouch, looking at this very bare military looking hallway. Which just meant it appeared to have been built in the fifties, complete with asbestos.

"Hang tight. I'll see what I can find." He wanted to kiss her, but even one moment would leave both of them and the man on the floor unprotected. A second was long enough for a bullet to be fired and one of them to end up dead.

Lord, help us.

EIGHTEEN

A piece of her heart went with him, disappearing through a door. Roxie looked down at the kid in front of her, some Marine trained to be nameless or faceless, just one in a sea of matching uniforms. But they were also trained to stand together. This kid sat alone in a hallway.

Abandoned.

"Don't worry." She reached for his wrist so she could feel for his pulse. "We'll get you—"

She cut herself off.

His eyes stared, sightless, at the wall over her shoulder.

She pressed two fingers to the underside of his jaw and held her breath for a second. Nothing. Roxie's lips puffed out.

She closed his eyes. "Sorry you didn't make it, kid."

Tears gathered, but she sniffed and blinked, not wanting to break down in a place like this. Maybe later, wrapped in Liam's arms, she could cry about the tragedy. Then she would have her taskforce teammates, or her friends at Vanguard, find out who this kid was so she could maybe visit his family. Tell them that he'd died a hero.

A tear rolled down her cheek. Defiant grief like the fire flickering in her midsection just thinking about what had happened here.

Lord, don't let this cost any more lives.

It wasn't a guarantee. But she needed that moment talking to God to help her get centered in this chaos.

Down the hall to her right, a door flung open so hard it slammed against the wall. Two armed men wired up with radios emerged like they were taking the last couple steps up a set of stairs, reaching the top. The basement level she'd seen evidence of? Beside the door, a keypad blinked red. As did the sights on their guns.

She didn't need to look down to see the red dots of their aim on the front of her shirt.

Roxie lifted her hands and realized she'd set her pistol on the floor. *Not good.*

"Hey! What are you—" The commander rounded the hall corner behind her, mid-yell. Gunfire burst down the hall. His body jerked, and one round embedded itself in his cheek. He hit the ground in a crumple of limbs.

Roxie's entire body tensed. Was her brain matter going to be on the wall behind her in a second?

She turned slowly.

The man in a white jumpsuit between four armed guys said, "Now. Get her."

Roxie flinched. There was no time to reach for her gun, and she would end up getting shot for it anyway.

"She comes with us."

Two of the men strode to her.

Roxie backed up a step. Then another. She nearly tripped over the legs belonging to that dead Marine but caught herself. The men grabbed her arms. She yelped. "Let go of me! Liam!"

She screamed his name a couple more times, as loud as she could, praying he heard her.

Or someone else.

These men were the intruders, and they were here for this man in the white jumpsuit now in front of her.

Carim Ismael Darwish sneered at her. "A treat for your trouble."

One of the men with him snickered.

"Let's go." Carim clapped.

"This way." The tone was dark and deadly in a way that made her shiver.

Roxie had gone up against an abusive ex who had tormented her until he decided to kill them both in a car accident after she told him she was leaving him. She'd crawled from the wreckage. His brother had come after her two years later. In the course of that, she'd come face to face with some dangerous Russians.

None of them even touched the level these guys were on.

There was a power and a lethality in their every movement that made her want to curl up and not breathe until it was over.

This was who her brother had aligned himself with? Whatever his reason, that wasn't a man she understood. And he was certainly nothing like the boy she'd known growing up.

Where was he?

They followed the hall to what seemed like another wing, and one of them opened a door. They descended another set of stairs into a darkened area.

Hadn't they come up from a lower level?

The men shoved her to one side with Darwish. He looked at her, but she didn't say any of the things in her mind. She should fight him. Slap him. Try to kill him. Alert someone, somehow. She didn't even have her phone. It wasn't in her pocket, so it had to have fallen out in the dirt.

All she had was her Marshal star.

Could she do some damage with that? Probably not enough to start a fight with a dangerous warlord and four men with guns.

Roxie shivered again. Where was Liam? Or a whole fire team of Marines who could rescue her? Or the National Guard? Or an army of some kind?

Anyone would do.

Because if these men got her in their vehicle, she might as well be dead. Or gone forever. And there was so much she wanted to do, like finding her brother and figuring things out with her friend Destiny. She and Liam needed to talk to Adam together, so they would both know what kind of man her brother was now. She didn't want to be swept along by her feelings, overwhelmed by the loss she'd felt for years, and Liam would help ground her.

Lord...

The mercenary guys killed two more Marines. One took a keycard and unlocked a heavy fire door. Beyond it was a concrete room with a ramp at the far end. Four SUVs, two on each side, were evidently their way out.

Two of the gunmen went to one vehicle. The other two loaded her and Darwish into another.

Roxie dragged her feet. She struggled. She tried to make it take as long as possible.

Someone rattled the door handle.

"Liam!" She screamed his name.

The mercenary shoved her head sideways, and her temple bounced off the back window. Pain exploded in her head.

Before she could go down, he lifted her and shoved her in the car.

Roxie landed sprawled on the seat, far too close to Darwish. She scrambled back and nearly got shut in the door. It slammed, the loud noise ringing in her ears.

It dissipated in time for her to hear Darwish chuckle, and they set off.

The driver gunned it, turning the vehicle as they accelerated.

She grabbed the handle at the top of the door. As soon as they straightened, she would—

Roxie let go of the handle long enough to buckle her seatbelt. The driver gunned it after the first SUV, up the ramp, out into the night...

Or not.

The ramp didn't emerge right away. They sped down a tunnel for at least half a mile before the SUV bumped up another incline, and they emerged outside.

She looked at the terrain around them, then twisted in her seat and looked out the back window. They'd exited the compound itself, leaving it behind as they headed along a dirt track, presumably back to the road.

Hope you know where I'm at, Liam.

She'd rather he found her alive than in pieces on the side of the road somewhere. Or buried in a shallow grave.

Lord, I need some help not falling into despair.

She was pretty good at worst case scenarios. Roxie wanted to believe that someone who'd been through all she had in her life didn't deserve to suffer more, but that wasn't the reality of the world she lived in. One that was inhabited by men like this.

Men who did whatever they wanted and hurt whoever they wanted in the first place—and didn't care one bit about the pain they caused.

No one followed them.

She kept looking behind to see rescue on its way.

Nothing.

If no one said anything, she was going to scream. "I guess you're pretty happy being out of there."

"Freedom has its perks."

"Same kind of perks you get being installed as the leader of a country?"

Carim chuckled. "Until America decides to do whatever they want." His tone soured. "Detaining a man without due process. As if I did not attend law school. It certainly wasn't so I could have my rights stripped away and be kept in the dark, subject to whatever torture my captors could conceive of. And they call us animals."

She wasn't going to get into an argument with him. There were things about the US that most of its citizens either didn't want to entertain. Or if they were aware of it, maybe they would encourage it—as long as it didn't affect their personal lives.

What she wanted was information about what

was going on. Except, did a man who had been in a black site with no access to the outside world know anything about what was going on?

She couldn't just sit here.

Roxie gripped the handle and tried to think. She said, "Are we going to meet General Darwish?" to the two guys in the front as much as to Carim.

No one answered.

"That's who hired you guys, right?" Why not go for broke? "Do you know Adam Helton? Any idea who he is? Adam Russell Helton?"

Neither man in front answered.

She was surprised they hadn't told her to shut up yet. Darwish hadn't slapped her. Maybe he couldn't because he lacked the strength. That would be satisfying. Maybe he was inert like a broken toy that no longer did what it was designed to do.

He'd been tossed away by the government.

Then again, they'd continued to extract information from him since his capture, so maybe he had his uses.

Roxie leaned her cheek on her bicep, still grasping the handle, and looked out the window. A few stars peeked through the clouds. She hadn't wished on a star for years, choosing instead to put her faith in the God who made those stars. And that was very different than wishing.

One star veered to the side.

She watched it, frowning. A plane? No, it was far too low. It had to be a chopper coming in. But was it Darwish coming to pick up his brother, or was it something else?

The guy in the front passenger seat said, "Copy that. I see it, coming in low at three o'clock."

They'd seen it, too.

The two SUVs veered off the dirt road, and the tires fought against loose, sandy dirt. They parked nearly at right angles with the road. "Everyone out."

She tried the handle, but it didn't work.

Locked in.

The two men in front chuckled. The driver said, "Except you."

The passenger got out, waiting with the door open. The sound of the helicopter came nearer, that steady beating of blades as Darwish swept low and readied the aircraft to land.

She watched the side door open and saw a muzzle flash.

The man in front of her jerked and went down. Roxie ducked her head by her knees, gasping. Gunfire pinged off the hood of the vehicle, shattered the window, and caught the driver in the neck. Blood sprayed back to hit Carim in the face.

Someone roared outside, and more gunfire exchanged with the weapon on the helicopter.

The need to run surged in her. Roxie didn't want to get shot so she couldn't climb in the front. She hit the button for the window, and it started to roll down. *Lord.* She had to get away from Carim when everything in her screamed that staying would be the end of her life.

She reached out the window for the handle on the outside. Light flashed over the opening where her window had been.

Carim grabbed her hair and pulled.

Roxie swung her fist back and slammed the base of her clenched hand into his nose. She heard the crunch, and he screamed, clutching his face. She scrambled out the door and fell onto the dirt on her hands and one knee, the other leg wedged in the car.

Carim grabbed her pant leg.

Roxie scrambled away, but he had a tight hold on her ankle. She screamed, but the sound disappeared in the noise of the helicopter. She kicked out again and again.

But Carim wouldn't let her go.

NINETEEN

Liam gasped for breath. His back hit the floor of the lower detainment level. This guy was so much bigger than the last one—and even bigger than Liam. He lifted both feet and slammed his boots into the guy's stomach.

The guy stumbled back two steps, laughing, and caught himself.

One foot raised to stomp on Liam.

He rolled to the side and came up, fists raised. Where his gun was, he had no idea. But no matter. This was far more satisfying anyway.

Where was Roxie?

He'd been supposed to find a medical wing or anything—or anyone—that might help take care of that kid upstairs. Prognosis wasn't looking good. As soon as he'd gone downstairs, he'd found a huge riot with all the doors open in the containment level. At least eight prisoners battled it out with the Marines, some of them fighting two on one. None of the Marines opened fire.

They had to have been ordered not to kill the prisoners.

Which meant whoever gave that order considered them too valuable to take their lives.

The prisoner who'd taken one look at Liam and rushed him did so again. Liam bobbed and weaved away from a punch and drove a hook into the guy's ribcage. His hand exploded with pain.

Sweat and some blood dripped into his eyes. He swiped it away with his sleeve and hooked his leg behind the man's. He didn't go down.

I need a plan.

A few feet away, one of the Marines, who held a fire extinguisher aloft, was knocked out by a punch. He fell to the floor, and the fire extinguisher rolled toward Liam.

He hit out at the man close to him again. A two punch-elbow combination his drill sergeant had taught him the hard way—through practicing it on Liam enough times he caught on and countered. The prisoner might be heavy as an oak, but he didn't know the counter move.

The guy stumbled back into another Marine, who kicked his boot down on the man's calf.

Liam swiped up the fire extinguisher and swung it around. He slammed the prisoner's head with the heavy metal. He collapsed to the floor, and Liam bent forward, breathing hard. He spotted Salty. "I need a medic."

"Lower floor in the other wing." Salty checked the pulse of the man he'd subdued. "This place is a maze so don't go looking for it on your own." He grabbed the man's feet. "Let's get them back in their cells, boys."

Liam figured his buddy meant him as well, so he hauled the tank-sized guy into a cell. Didn't matter if it was the right one. This place might be a maze, but what he wanted was to find Roxie. It had been far too long since he left her in that hallway with a dying man and came down here only to get tangled up in a fight.

Salty touched the radio on his collar. "Control, this is detainment. Shut the doors."

A second later, a buzzer resounded down the hall. Eight doors, four on each side, swung closed on their own. One had been empty.

"Who should be in the last one?" Liam pointed.

"Bro, you don't have clearance to be down here. No way I'm telling you that even if I did know." Salty motioned to the stairs. "Time to move."

"You're kicking me out? My wife is upstairs with one of your Marines, hanging on for dear life to what's left of his. They need help. That's why I came down here."

"Appreciate your assistance back there, but we don't need help." Salty stomped up the stairs behind him. Liam was about to counter with a reality check when Salty said, "Say again."

Liam paused on the stairs to glance back. Salty's face had paled.

"Copy that. I'm on my way." He started to climb the stairs before he realized Liam hadn't moved. "Go. We've got a breach in the garage."

"Not until you explain." Roxie could hold her own in that hall for a few more seconds, right? He didn't like how long it had been, so he tugged out his phone and called hers. "I wanna know what's going on. Forget about clearance. You know you can trust me." The phone started to ring, but she didn't pick up. Liam stared at his buddy until he didn't want to wait any longer. She wasn't answering.

He hung up. Time to go find her.

"We have four vehicles. Two left the garage level."

"Let me guess," Liam said. "The other wing?"

Salty didn't justify that with an answer. He simply said, "Time to find the captain, and we can go check it out. You can take your wife and leave the way you came. Nice to see you and all that." He reached around Liam for the door handle and stepped first into the hallway.

Ground level.

The same way Liam had come down. How many wings were there in this place? He didn't think he'd have been able to handle this kind of detail. He'd gone home to become a police officer after his father died for a reason. Not just because he wanted to follow in his father's footsteps, but because he'd always known deep down that he would end up doing that job.

He'd simply avoided the concept long enough to make his own way in the Corps for a while.

"Captain!" Salty jogged to a Marine on the floor, blood pooled around him.

"There's another as well." It was the man Roxie had been with. Pale, and his eyes closed. Liam didn't need to check for a pulse to see if he was dead. "She must've been ambushed." He straightened, turning around to scan both hallways, as if the threat would appear now.

He spotted her gun on the floor. Discarded. Or she'd been forced to drop it.

"Where are you?" He pulled out his phone again,

dialing with it low at his chest, but he didn't hear it ringing anywhere. When it went to voice mail this time, he left a message. "Call me back, Rox."

He wanted to offer a stern warning that she'd better not be in any danger, but it could very well be too late for that. "What were you saying about the garage?"

Salty straightened. "This is on you. If you hadn't been here, we wouldn't have been on the hill talking to you when the compound was breached."

"How about we finish resolving this issue before we unpack whose fault it was?" Considering this was a black site, he didn't think he'd end up in court. It wasn't like the case could be on public record. Liam scanned the hall again, then spotted a unit high in the corner of the wall. *Bingo.* "We need to look at that footage to find out what happened up here."

"I'm headed that way. Whether you follow or not is up to you and how many charges you want to be facing." Salty set off, striding past Liam.

"I'm not leaving without my wife. So help me find her quickly, and I'll be out of your hair. You can go search for Carim Ismael Darwish yourself without the help of my connected taskforce."

Salty glanced over his shoulder, and Liam caught the look on his face. He wanted help. He knew he was in over his head, with his captain dead.

"Sorry about your C.O."

"Let's find Anne."

Liam didn't bother explaining that she went by the Roxie end of Roxanne these days. He just wanted to find her.

Salty grabbed a key card from his sleeve and swiped it across the panel beside the door. The mechanism clicked, and he entered the control room. Two soldiers in uniform sat on swivel chairs at a wall of monitors.

"Everyone accounted for except one."

The man on the left nodded. "Darwish is gone."

Liam's stomach rolled. "I should call my team. Tell them he escaped custody, probably to meet up with his brother."

The second soldier turned, and he realized the redhead was a woman. She lifted her chin. On the desk, she had a mug that read *Make tea not war*.

"Did you see a woman in the hallway where the captain was shot?" And why hadn't they left this room to intervene and help? Unless they'd been ordered to stay here under any and all circumstances. "My wife is out there."

"Footage was down while we rebooted it to clear off the cyber attack they used to gain access. They knew they didn't have much time, but it was enough to get the prisoner from eight out. They must have breached somehow, or paid off someone with a badge to get in. They accessed the system from the inside and killed our security. It's all clear now, but the brass won't be happy."

"Can you pull up the live images?"

She frowned. "All I've got is the garage tunnel footage. By the time it came back online, the two vehicles were nearly to the exit."

"Show me?"

Salty shifted. Probably wanted to object. So what if Liam sounded and was acting like the cop—and federal agent—he was? The result on the case would be success.

Or he would die trying.

The marine clacked keys, and the screen closest to her flickered to a dark tunnel with lights overhead. Headlights filled the screen. "Hang on. There's another angle." She clicked again, and then moved the roller wheel on her mouse, and another image filled the screen.

An SUV passed from left to right in a blur. Moving fast. Determined to escape.

"There." Two vehicles, and he spotted something in one of the windows. A flash of blonde.

She paused it, then scrolled back, stopping on the rear window. Roxie had the handle at the top of the door in one hand, showing off the muscles in her arms. But the fear on her face stood in stark contrast to her strength.

It didn't matter how much physical toughness she had.

She was terrified.

Everything in him tensed nearly to the breaking point. "Where are they now?"

"We already sent a squad after the vehicles. As soon as they could rally, a team took off on ATVs to go after them."

Liam's jaw hurt he clenched it so hard. "You didn't answer my question."

"We are taking care of it."

A sharp beep sounded, followed by talking too garbled by crackling to be understandable. The other Marine at the desk swung around and grabbed a radio off the desktop. "Say again."

More crackling answered him.

Then a voice cut through. "...some kind of device."

"Repeat your last, over."

"...we tracked them...found a bomb." Silence echoed in the control room, and then the voice said, "The compound is set to blow."

The Marines froze.

Liam grabbed the radio. "Everyone out! Get out! Get out!"

He dropped it and ran for the door, skidding out into the hallway at a breakneck pace. He pounded down the hall toward the exterior door, ready to shove out and get free. Trying to convince himself that there was nothing he could do. Which was true. But leaving anyone behind didn't sit right.

He'd done it with Roxie and that young Marine. Now the kid was dead, and she was gone.

If he didn't get out of here, he would never be able to find her.

Their future would be over before it had ever really started.

Two steps from the door, the building exploded out from the middle. A Marine coming from the other direction was shoved up into the air by the blast. He hit the ceiling, and the interior wall collapsed down and then in on itself. The whole building compressed back in for a split second, like an inhale before the biggest exhale ever.

The structure exploded out in fire and force.

Taking Liam with it.

TWENTY

In the distance, a fireball exploded into the sky. Roxie scrambled to her feet and took two steps, racing after it. Wind from the helicopter rotors whipped her hair around her head, obscuring her vision. She wasn't going to be waylaid though.

Liam was back there.

She knew that now, just as she knew Darwish hadn't been in that helicopter. It hadn't landed yet. And when it did, there would be nothing she could do about what happened next.

All she could do was *run*.

Roxie got ten or so steps when someone slammed into her back. She hit the ground, a cloud of dirt puffing up into her face, and she had to cough. He tugged at her clothing, and she tried to push him off. Roxie shoved against the ground, her mind trying to figure out what he was even trying to do in front of the helicopter guys.

She screamed out all her desperate frustration, got purchase with one boot in the dirt, and pushed. The toe of the boot dug in, and she flung Carim to the side. Roxie rolled with him and used her momentum to slam her elbow into his face. Into his already broken nose.

Carim bellowed with rage.

Roxie swung her boot up over his body, aiming for his chin. He grabbed her shin and ankle. She wiggled, trying to get her leg free of his grip. He tried to drag her closer to him, hatred in his eyes and blood running down his face.

The helicopter touched down, shaking the ground.

Carim stared past her, the evil in his expression cracking a little. His grasp lightened.

Someone yelled, "Let her go!" in a language that wasn't English, but her brain couldn't remember what it was, even while she remembered what enough of the words meant that she understood him.

She scrambled back from Carim, but her limbs didn't want to coordinate with each other or her mind. Her arm gave out, and her back slammed onto the ground. *Liam.* She needed her phone. She needed to be back at the compound because it had just exploded, and he was still there.

Wasn't he?

Boots hit the ground.

She flinched, seeing more than one man approach. Dark in the dark night. Flashlight beams whipped across her vision, blinding her for a second. Someone dropped a water bottle beside her hip and ordered, "Drink."

No empathy. No compassion.

She wasn't going to be shot if she was being offered a drink. But they also didn't seem to be here to rescue her. Roxie drank half the bottle and sat up.

Carim still lay on the ground. He turned to one

side and spat blood on the ground. "You think I'm scared."

"I know you are." The man standing over him had a wool cap over his face, obscuring everything but that command presence. He would kill Carim absolutely, in a single heartbeat span, without even thinking about it. Whether he felt like he had to or if he wanted to didn't matter. He would just squeeze that trigger.

"Where's Darwish, Carim?" She took another drink. "He was going to meet you. Where?"

"You think I know? I have been in prison for years."

The man standing over him said, "Don't talk to her like that."

Someone else shifted, but with all the dark and the masks, she couldn't get a read on these guys at all. Geez, she'd thought the men in the car were lethal. These guys were on another level.

"He needs to give me intel, or all this was for *nothing*."

Someone close to her huffed what might've been a laugh. "You and me both, darlin'."

The guy by Carim glanced over his shoulder. "Bro, go do something useful."

"That's what I *am* doing."

"This has been great and all," Roxie managed to say as she clambered to her feet. "But I'll be taking that SUV now. You can tie Carim up in the back, and I'll return him to the marines."

Someone snorted.

"Care to tangle with the Northwest Counter Terrorism Taskforce?" She nearly put her hand on her hip.

"No, ma'am. I would not. I've heard enough about them."

"And who are you guys?" She glanced around.

The guy by Carim moved around him so that he could face her without losing sight of the man on the ground. "They didn't tell you?"

She shook her head. "My husband was back there." She waved the water bottle at the smoldering compound and managed to splash an arc of water. "I need to go find him. Make sure he is all right so we can get back to work on this case."

The man by Carim just stared at her. "You want to go back to him?"

His friend said, "It's worse than we thought."

"Look," Roxie said, certain there was something here she was seriously missing. "I have a job to do."

"Because you're a US Marshal now." The man by Carim grinned a flash of white teeth in the dark night. "I heard about that."

She still had her star on her belt, so that was probably how he knew. "Carim goes with me."

"Sorry, sweetheart. No can do." The man closest to her stepped in front of her, blocking her view of Carim and the man over there. "Do us all a favor and come with us."

She took a step back.

The last time a group of tough guys had forced her to go with them, it had been for their purposes. That wasn't going to happen. Not when she needed to get to Liam.

And not ever, in fact.

"That's cute. She thinks she has a choice."

Roxie didn't know who said that, but the intent was clear.

The one in front of her said, "You wanna stop Carim's brother from fulfilling his plan? Then work with us. Put all that know-how and all your connections in the pot with us, and we'll get it done. It's time to work together."

"I don't even know who you guys are." Except that the one farthest back was the man who'd sliced up Liam behind the barn.

This was the team who'd chased them?

As if she would leave her husband and go with them. They couldn't possibly think the taskforce would join forces with some nameless faceless group that certainly wasn't military or even special ops. They were more like the mercenaries who had busted out Carim than the good guys.

The man lowered one hand in a fist showing her the inside of his forearm, where he had the tattoo of the word *Renegades* stretching from his elbow to his wrist.

Her time at Vanguard Security and Investigations flashed back to a company email she'd seen. It had been in a chain, where someone had been talking to Peter. Some team he'd done a rotation with while training as an operative. A top-secret black ops division of the company.

Vanguard Renegades.

No one outside of the company should know they even existed.

She didn't work for them anymore, so she lifted her chin. "Is that supposed to mean something to me?"

They stared at her.

Roxie stepped back a couple more paces. "Are you taking Carim?"

The man standing over the bad guy choked out the word, "Yes."

"And you're working this case?"

He nodded.

"And you'll call my office if there are leads to run down so we can follow up officially, run down things maybe you might not have access to. Work a different angle." She just wanted to get out of here, and that kind of official/unofficial division of labor was all she could think of.

Roxie swiped tears from her face, not even sure why she was crying. "I have to go."

The man cleared his throat. "So go."

She stumbled between them, toward the hood of the car.

"Take this." One handed her a business card with a phone number on it and no name. On the back were gold letters embossed, just VR. Nothing else.

She had to brace herself on the hood of the car to keep her balance. Had to tug the dead guy out of the way in order to climb in.

Roxie didn't look at them when she turned the engine back on. She fixed the seat position so she could reach the pedals, adjusted the mirror, and put the SUV in gear. Then she glanced over, pulling out, already leaving. Already turning around in the road.

She pressed down on the gas pedal, probably spraying dirt and dust behind her.

Liam.

It took far longer to get back there and figure out how to get through the emergency vehicles. She spotted someone in a fire department coat with CHIEF on the back and left the vehicle idling so she could run over. "Excuse me! Excuse me!"

He spun, a good looking African American man probably in his fifties. She stumbled, and he caught her elbows. "Where did you come from?"

"I was in there with my husband, but we got separated." She had to gasp. "He's blond. He has a ponytail." That alone would distinguish him from all the military guys.

"Right." The chief nodded. "We pulled out a guy with a ponytail and a badge."

"Homeland Security?"

That had been a test, and she got the answer right. He nodded. "You should talk to the police."

"Where is he?" She gripped his forearms. "Tell me. Please."

The man's expression softened. Behind him was pure chaos, people and destruction, flames, and the spray of hoses. "He was already transported to the hospital. He was hurt pretty badly."

"Which hospital?"

As soon as he said the name, she took off running. In the car, she managed to get the name in the search bar with only three tries. Fifteen minutes later, she pulled up outside the busy city hospital, thankfully not far from the freeway exit.

She parked across two spaces, not even bothering to lock the car or take the keys with her. Roxie slammed the door, crying out when various aches and pains made themselves known.

She forced her body to walk all the way to the front entrance. Find the reception desk. No point not trying to look like someone who'd seen more than one man die, been kidnapped, fought for her life, and now made it all the way here. She was covered in dirt, sweating through her clothes, and probably bleeding.

The desk attendant blinked, then slid her glasses from the string around her neck onto her nose. "It's going to be about a twenty minute wait to see a doctor."

"Liam O'Connell."

She blinked. "Excuse me."

"I'm here to see Liam O'Connell. He was transported here a short while ago. He was in an explosion."

The woman said, "Are you a relation?"

"I'm his wife." Roxie held up her left hand, as though the plain silicone band was enough to prove what she said.

"You said O'Connell?"

"Liam. Lee. Or maybe he's a John Doe? He didn't have his wallet or ID, just the metal badge." He must've had his phone, though. Did the staff here know who he was?"

"There was a John Doe brought in, since I can't find your husband's name. He was unfortunately pronounced dead as a result of his injuries. I'm sure you can take a look and confirm for us if it's the person you're looking—"

Roxie stumbled back.

...pronounced dead...

She turned, blindly seeking something. She didn't know what.

She clipped a guy walking past, mumbled an apology, and stumbled to the nearest exit. Before she slammed into the doors, they swept open, and the night air gusted in.

A circular driveway was lined with people and vehicles. Roxie passed them, ignoring anyone who tried to talk to her.

She found a dark, secluded alcove just past the pickup curb and stopped. Her shoulder slammed the wall, the bumpy stucco cutting into her skin.

She slid all the way down to sit on the ground, crying out at the sting.

Warmth trickled down the outside of her arm.

She didn't know how long she sat there, gasping sobs she didn't know how to control. Then someone crouched. Fingers touched her knee. She flinched.

"It's me, Sis." He shifted, and she saw Adam's face flash in the glow of a yellow streetlight. "The boys said they saw you with Carim."

She sobbed, trying to speak. Finally, she managed to say, "Liam's dead."

Adam slid his arms under her and lifted her. She thought she heard the word "Good" and started to struggle against his hold on her. "No. Don't." She gasped. *Liam.* She wanted Liam, not this.

But Adam didn't let her go.

KEEP READING FOR...

- What to read next.

- Where to find it.

ABOUT THE AUTHOR

Find out more about Lisa Phillips at her website, where you'll discover more romantic suspense fan-favorite series and heart-pounding thriller novels.
https://authorlisaphillips.com

If you loved this book, please consider sharing about it on social media, or leaving a review on Lisa's website. Your review will help others find great books to entertain and encourage them!

For a FREE novel from Lisa Phillips, scan the QR code below with your phone camera to connect to Lisa's newsletter and be the first to hear about sales, new books, and recommendations for your TBR pile.

- facebook.com/authorlisaphillips
- instagram.com/lisaphillipsbks
- bookbub.com/authors/lisa-phillips

ALSO BY LISA PHILLIPS

Benson First Responders is part of the Last Chance County universe, and several other connected series. Head over to Lisa's website to find a chronological reading timeline to find what to read next!

Find out more about Benson First Responders on Lisa's website:

https://authorlisaphillips.com/